A
Cottonwood
Stand

A Cottonwood Stand

A Novel of Nebraska

Chuck Redman

SUNSTONE
PRESS

SANTA FE

Sunstone books may be purchased for educational, business, or sales promotional use.
For information please write: Special Markets Department, Sunstone Press,
P.O. Box 2321, Santa Fe, New Mexico 87504-2321.

Cover artwork by Rebecca Redman and Joshua Redman
Book and cover design › Vicki Ahl
Body typeface › Goudy Old Style
Printed on acid-free paper
∞
eBook 978-1-61139-545-7

Library of Congress Cataloging-in-Publication Data

Names: Redman, Chuck, 1952- author.
Title: A cottonwood stand : a novel of Nebraska / by Chuck Redman.
Description: Santa Fe : Sunstone Press, 2018.
Identifiers: LCCN 2018001294 (print) | LCCN 2018004602 (ebook) | ISBN
    9781611395457 | ISBN 9781632932204 (softcover : alk. paper)
Subjects: LCSH: Country life--Nebraska--Fiction.
Classification: LCC PS3618.E43435 (ebook) | LCC PS3618.E43435 C68 2018
    (print) | DDC 813/.6--dc23
LC record available at https://lccn.loc.gov/2018001294

WWW.SUNSTONEPRESS.COM
SUNSTONE PRESS / POST OFFICE BOX 2321 / SANTA FE, NM 87504-2321 /USA
(505) 988-4418 / ORDERS ONLY (800) 243-5644 / FAX (505) 988-1025

To Jilla, Josh and Rebecca

Preface

I'm a Nebraskan, born and raised. I love my native state and I admire its people, both ancient and present. But I'm saddened by much of what we call progress and how it has transformed the place so fundamentally over time. Like everywhere else, Nebraska has become modernized, urbanized, and homogenized. Though less developed than other parts of the country, still a lot of its history and charm have been plowed under and paved over. No one sets out intentionally to spoil the environment, but that seems to be the chief legacy whenever there is cutting, drilling, or building upon our land.

Moliere said it so well: "It is a vigorous blow to vices," he wrote in his Preface to *Tartuffe*, "to expose them to laughter. Criticism is taken lightly, but men will not tolerate satire. They are quite willing to be mean, but they never like to be ridiculed."
In full agreement with that philosophy, this book is simply my one attempt to look at Nebraska and to mildly satirize the things that ought to be satirized and honor the things that ought to be honored. There are many of both.

Part of the idea for the book came from the town where I live, in southern California. It's a town that is committed to protecting its native oak trees. Many of its oak trees, especially the California Valley Oaks, are so big and so beautiful that you just want to stand there and look up and smile. Some are hundreds of years old. Imagine what it was like four or five hundred years ago when they were just starting out. Imagine all the good and bad things that have passed under their branches. They are still here, these trees, part of our community, but it's a community and a region where commerce and development, not trees, are the kings.

I started to think about the possibility that someday these stately oaks might all be chopped down to make way for more freeways, malls or luxury residential tracts. I wondered if someday the last oak tree in town might look around itself and know that it would soon be a pile of firewood at somebody's hillside mansion. I thought about these things but I realized that Nebraska was the place that I really wanted to write about, and that I was still "rooted" to my small town past, growing up in the very center of the country. So instead of the oak tree, it's the cottonwood. And these cottonwoods are nurtured by the Platte River and rich Nebraska soil. And they have been for hundreds of years. And the result, especially on a morning of sunshine and treetop winds, is memorable.

I once saw the inside of a meatpacking plant. The head of the plant took me all through the facility. I hadn't been quite honest with the gentleman about where I was coming from, philosophically. Afterwards I wrote down everything I could remember. And waited for the smell to clear out from my nostrils. There's some part of my brain that is still trying to get out of that plant. Meatpacking plants like that have been sprouting up in small towns all over Nebraska and neighboring states. Those towns are forever changed by the rapid growth and problems that follow. Problems, I'm afraid, that are even bigger than giant cottonwoods.

Most books are labors of love. This labor was made lovelier by the people who read my manuscript at various stages and gave me such needed encouragement and advice at all points along the way: the incredible writers Brad Chisholm and Claire Kim, who read my manuscript on an airplane and didn't throw it out the window and told me some of the nicest things a writer could ever want to hear. Pat Walsh, who was the first publishing professional to take the time to talk to me about the business and to give me some real hope of finding a publisher. My niece Sarah Scheerger, whose writing career has inspired me and who has given me invaluable advice about publishing and keeping your sanity.

My sisters Pat, Nancy and Beth, who spoiled me as a kid and who still manage to lift my spirits, even when I thrust upon them my roughest and lamest of first drafts. Their husbands Ralph, Larry and Steve, who are collectively such a wealth of knowledge and advice that who needs the internet?

No writing or, for that matter, getting up every day would have much meaning or purpose if it weren't for my best readers: Jilla, my wife, Rebecca, my daughter, and Josh, my son. What they've taught me about life and how to live it would make the greatest book in the world, but there aren't the words to do it justice.

Sunday

*F*or the life of me, I cannot decide whether ambivalence is a good thing or a bad thing.

When was the last time you sat down on your best davenport and tried to hash that thorny problem out in your head? It don't get any more basic than that. If you want to live a life of principle. Which is what folks nowadays could use a good dose of.

Now look here, I'm not out to bad-mouth everybody in town, and I don't say it weren't a nice graduation and all. The feller who give the main talk and brought fame to the school thirty-six years ago when he become Deputy Undersecretary of Agriculture under Ford was a speck long-winded, no question. But the convocation as a whole was generally pretty agreeable for the most part.

Fact is I always choke up just a little to see them tiny seedlings that I've watched get growed up over the years, and here they are graduating high school, looking awful proud and accomplished. One hundred and eight flushed young faces, all told, decked out in blue. Class of 2010. Where'd them years go? Gee, couldn't help but feel just a shade sorry there for little Caylie Hauptman—yessir, dad's Phil Hauptman, farms down across the river—when her cap blew off at the "rocket's red glare" and she dropped her microphone. But the way she kept her cool and almost hit that high note was most inspiring. A trouper ain't she.

I hate like the deuce to see a happy occasion like this go all sour and bitter. But I'm afraid that's the way it's sittin for the Portillo family. Tanya and her folks ain't talkin now. I expect that'll last til at least dessert at Pavarotti's where Tanya and her best friend Keith O'Connor (just a friend friend, as they say) decided to have their graduation dinner. It's a dang shame, too, specially after Tanya give such a beautiful co-valedictory speech entitled "Look How Far We've Come in 168 Short Years." Well, Tanya did kinda throw the fat in the fire.

"Mom and Dad," she up and announces, still smiling pretty two seconds after they took her and Keith's picture outside the football stadium, "tomorrow I'm going to City Hall and get a petition to run for City Council in the primary. The one coming up? I think I'd be a pretty good councilperson, and I'm eighteen now." She's took off the commencement cap and her red hair is crispy in the late sun and wind. She's got a glow about her.

Mom's sunburnt face looks as though her heart has just sank like a water well in the sandhills—which moms' hearts do when anything goes haywire respectin their kids. Dad's face looks like a few choice words are suddenly bangin on his teeth to get out, and his smile ain't the kind you take pictures of. "Honey," says Brent Portillo, with a kinda forced dad voice way down deep, "you just graduated high school. Don't start going overboard on us."

"Dad, all my friends who are eighteen will vote for me. Plus, anyone who's not totally reactionary and wants some change in this—"

"Honey," he says, brushing two or three dead gnats off his shiny forehead, "you're going to college in the fall, you won't even be here." There's a small tussle going on between Keith and his mom over the letter that says he graduated and the diploma will come in the mail in two to four weeks, and if it don't there's a number to call. She's saying Keith is wrinkling the letter, which he kinda is, and he's saying it don't matter it's not the diploma it's just a form letter and after a couple more seconds of wrangling between them two the letter rips clean up the middle. Mrs. O'Connor's hankie, though it's real lacy all around, don't look nearly absorbent enough for the situation.

Anyways Tanya's been thinking, she owns up at last to her folks, of maybe just going to the community college over in Grand Island. Live at home and commute.

"Oh, sweetheart," cries Mom, "you worked so hard to get straight A's, you've got that wonderful scholarship to Lincoln—"

"I don't care, Mom, I wanna do something that really—"

"You just better care," Dad growls over his daughter's poor pleadin voice, "after all we've done. Or I'll pomp your circumstance, young lady."

With Brent Portillo's green eyes, just a shade darker than his daughter's, we might as well be lookin at two hungry cats and one bowl of chow.

"Not funny, Dad," and that was the last that was spoke, as I said. Now, as Sinatra sings in the background, Mom's just kinda pokin at her Alfredo, Dad looks like his veal Parmesan is stuck somewheres in the rib area, the O'Connors is all just lookin down at their plates and gulping their food like they're gettin charged by the half-hour. Tanya—she ain't touched a drop. Her shoulders is stiff and from the way she's starin at her feta and arugula you'd think they was last month's science project. You want principle? Tanya's clinched mouth—it's about as serious as Sittin Bull with a loaded shotgun and Custer's personal address in his headband.

Monday

*T*he *Cottonwood Caterwauler* is kicking up dust like a stampede of bison. I oughta know. When dust gets kicked around, I tend to take it somewhat personal. Anyways, I ain't mad. She's hands-down the last bastion and beacon of independent journalism in the whole Outstate area, the *Caterwauler*. She knows an issue when she spots one. And this here, this is an issue. The paper's motto—"We Go Out on a Limb for You!"—those aren't just hollow words.

I call her *She*, but that's fitting. A newspaper's just a thing, it don't think or feel about the problems of the day, not quite like a human. But in the case of the *Caterwauler* she's a *She* all right, since the editor and owner is Janet Hinderson and—well, let's just say that Janet has opinions on things that are a little stronger than Apache rawhide. And a bit of a—by golly, I better just watch what I say. I sure don't want you to git the wrong idea.

Anyways, Janet ain't the commie pinko hippy radical that some Cottonwoodians claim she is. It's been whispered that once upon a time she was registered Republican, up until Iran-Contra, and that she'd gone out and voted for Reagan and Bush in '84. But Janet matured into a moderate, which in Outstate Nebraska means not Republican. She agonized over Obamacare, but she finally come out one and a half thumbs up in favor. That was some jim dandy editorial she plastered the town with back in that day.

So it ain't no surprise that Janet's sittin right now, hammering out a socko editorial—brassy as a dang trumpet section. There ain't gonna be no doubt in no one's mind which way the *Caterwauler* is comin down on Zoning Petition 17 and Council Motion 188.

Dogs trained to never bark. Little kids taught from birth that you can't never cry out loud, no matter what life tosses at you. The entire human flock livin in humble villages where share and share alike is the creed. The spirit of brotherhood at its best, you might say. Money? That evil commodity ain't been invented and ain't no call for it. A little friendly bartering does the job just fine.

"Rabbit and fox okay?"

"Nope."

"All my fingers?"

"Toes, too."

"Left foot or right?"

"Both."

"Shake."

And simple as that, puffing on a soothing pipeful of tobacco and willow bark, Chief Rain Bear has just got himself a nice new wife. Number three if you happen to be keeping track. He's agreed to fork over as many buffalo robes as he's got fingers and toes. A fair price for the adopted daughter of Eats No Breakfast, a big proud-looking gent sitting cross-legged, with four quail feathers in his long parted hair.

And Eats won't let the Chief forget about saving him a front row seat at all the council fires. Plus, the groom'll be throwing in a pair of beaded moccasins for everyone in the bride's teepee. "And she's worth every bead," adds Eats. "Haven't you always heard me admit she's a better daughter than my own flesh and blood child? You won't regret it for even one beat of a hummingbird's wing."

"What if she balks?" And Chief Rain Bear lays his pipe down alongside the low fire of dry buffalo chips in the center of the snug teepee.

Well, Eats No Breakfast poo-poos that silly notion and insists the gal's as mild-mannered as a newborn fawn. And with a face that suddenly looks like it just give birth, he pulls a rawhide strip from around his neck and hands it over to Rain Bear. "Here, take my wolftooth choker. You're my son now." And Eats' big lower lip starts in atrembling something fearsome.

Chief Rain Bear, who has gray hair and was already scalping worthy enemies long before Eats No Breakfast was even slid out into the painted fingers of a smiling midwife, stares at the four pearly fangs dangling from his grasp. He don't know what to say at the moment, he just gapes in admiration at his brand new papa. And these two happy gents start slapping each other on the back, chuckling and guffawing like parrots and recounting stories of brave exploits they've both heard more often than they could tell you.

Yessir, don't think fer a minute things was always the way they is nowadays. It's nice to recollect back to this here band of friendly folk called the Oglala Sioux, couple three hundred years before the covered wagons and pony soldiers come along. The Sioux back in them days was way outnumbered by the buffalo, but that's how they liked it. These Oglala folks moved around some. But you could say they was pretty much at home up northwest a ways across the sandhills from where this here town of Cottonwood sits today.

Now these Oglala was a hard-workin hard-livin band of kinfolk, with a tradition like you wouldn't believe. And they never done me one speck of harm, no more than the antelopes nor the coyotes done. And I'm talkin more years than even I can count, goin back many winters as they would of put it themselves in one of their handed-down campfire stories.

I wish you could of seen with your own eyes how them folks made a pretty respectable life for theirselves. Without all the newfangled—well, now don't get me started down that path. At any rate, there they'd be, camped in just the right spot against one of my grassy hillocks near a river or little feedin creek with a few poplars, cottonwoods and willows alongside. And being it's a cool spring morning with dry silky air and racing clouds above, daily chores is the order of the day. The Oglala is a anthill of activity, make your head spin. Motley dogs is tearing around after scraps, not barking but snarling low at one another whenever they get the urge. Little bitty kids is toddlin around aimless, watching the gals at work. Nary a one of them tykes is crying so much as a single boo. Some of the gals—and there are plenty—is pounding on dried chunks of buffalo meat with wild berries mixed in. Others is sewing, mending skins, stirring pots. And most of the guys what ain't out huntin is cuttin lodgepoles out of cottonwood or fashioning arrowheads out of flintrock with stone knives. Or maybe arrangin marriages like our two friends you just heard about. Some kind of holy man is telling stories with a lot of hand gestures to a couple older potbellied fellas sittin on stacks of hides. One young feller is walking around on his hands in moccasins, believe it or not, with his feet straight in the air and a fake face affixed to his heels. This feller's known as a Contrary and, as a sorta self-punishment for some dishonorable act, he does everything backwards so's you almost get used to seeing that mask coming at you like it was any regular joe.

From the grassy flats across the creek comes a small cluster of young gals, toting stacks of buffalo chips in satchels made of skin of the same critter. The gals is laughing amongst themselves, not paying no attention to a gang of boys in breechcloth playin mock ambush and capture near the creekbank. One of the gals, who you could call Running Water, for that's her everyday name but not her true unspoken name, suddenly stops laughing and turns to her companion near to tears. With her braided head hangin low and shoulders slouched, she's awhimpering softly about somethin pretty tragic, having some reference to ending up married to old Chief Rain Bear. "Of all the girls on the plains, why did he hafta pick me!" The gal she moans this to has long black hair thick as a jungle, angled in the westerly wind. Her you could call Lark Laying Eggs.

This Lark, stopping to shift her load of buffalo chips to the other shoulder, promptly counsels that when the Chief shows up with his hides and second-rate moccasins, Running Water should inform their Pop that she downright objects to marrying the cranky old lizard. "What does he need three—" Whoosh! The two gals flinch as a blunt-ended toy arrow comes whipping between them and plunks into the heavy brush to their rear. They look toward the creek but all there is is some suspicious ripples in the water and air bubbles poppin to the surface.

"I can't," laments Running Water, reminding Lark how much their Pop's counting on this marriage to boost his status. "You know how he wants to become a council chief, and join the Kit Fox Society."

Lark looks a little ticked off at this and, with a rising tide of emotion, she up and declares that the two of them gals must run away from their village, and seek a better life with Running Water's people, the Pawnee. She tells her sister about the last straw, which was yesterday when she asked their Pop if she could speak at tomorrow's Council Fire. "And he gave me that look, you know the one. 'Lark,' he says, 'this is a war council. It's either go to war or sit home weaving potholders.' He said you and I can bring round the sage tea, but not a word may we utter. So I start arguing. That's not fair, I told him, our scalps are on the line just like you braves. He got so upset," and here Lark Laying Eggs shows an expression of pain as if she has personally did exactly what her name conveys, "he covers his ears and starts moaning. All about having a daughter who drives men away the minute she opens her mouth, and who by the way isn't getting any younger."

Running Water can't help but shake her head and wince up at her sister. She admits she heard their Pop yowling 'Bad Medicine' yesterday sometime after everyone (but him) finished breakfast.

Lark raises her eyebrows. "He went off somewhere to build a sweat lodge so he could purify something or other before the Great Spirit." Fine, she says, she's through being pigeonholed. The two of them will run, and no looking back.

Running Water shakes her head and her deep-set eyes dilate. "I haven't got your nerve. I'm Sioux now, the Pawnee wouldn't know me from a stray rabbit."

"You were captured from them, they'd be out of their minds with joy to get you back."

"It's too late." Just off to the north now a young brave goes by the name of Lean Wolf comes over the nearest rise, carrying the carcass of a half-growed elk across his back and smiling in their direction with teeth like the Rocky Mountains. Running Water nods in his direction. "He won't let you go."

"It's none of his affair," and with her pretty nose held high and uppity against the cool breeze, Lark says she'd sooner marry the slimiest frog on that creekbank. Then she looks at Running Water like she just now realizes there's a flesh and blood person standin there. Says she can't believe she won't have her sis to talk to. "Who's supposed to listen to all my gripes?" Lark pert'ner breaks down, which Oglala gals generally save for funerals only. But she recovers and points her finger at her adopted sister like a warning. "We'll be together soon, R.W., for good. In a better place. Understood?" Droppin her load of chips on the ground, Lark's thick mantle of hair wraps round the sloping shoulders of Running Water, who she hugs with all the warmth of real true-blood kin.

So what in blazes are Zoning Petition 17 and Council Motion 188? Well guess what, mister. That big company out of Omaha? Euphemion Packing Company? You know, the one with the slogan "I like a good steak." They're jockeying right this minute to put one of their local meatpacking plants in this here little town of Cottonwood. And, exactly where do you suppose they resolved to put that facility? Smack dab, and I'll be damned, on top of the oldest stand of cottonwood trees in town—in fact in the whole Platte Valley.

Now I ain't no lawyer, but here goes. Article 7 of the Cottonwood City Charter provides as follows (I'm quotin' verbatim here):

"It shall be unlawful to remove, relocate, cut, or encroach into the protected zone of any cottonwood tree, unless expressly permitted by the full Council upon a showing of an immediate danger to the health, safety or welfare of one or more residents."

You see the issue now, my friend?

So, how'd this little town end up lovin cottonwoods so much? Seems that's how it got sprung up in the first place: Them early pioneers on the Oregon Trail was pretty dang relieved when they got to this bend in the Platte River and run right into a stand of cottonwoods gianter than they'd ever seen, surrounded by about the richest soil on earth (I can't take no credit—it was ol' Water and Weather what done it). Well, they named the biggest, eldest tree Old Grateful, which they was. So the little town of Cottonwood got sprung up, and they made sure them cottonwoods was protected.

Well, I'll stop yammering. Starting to feel a little parched in the gullet. My aquifer's drying up, you know. I remember them old times, though. When water wasn't no issue, I was as free as a lazy hawk, no fences and no boundaries. Now I'm treated like dirt, but don't you ever call me that. You might as well call me Nebraska. That's what people around these parts call me.

Now this issue is no small hay to the 8,716 people of Cottonwood. In fact, those're the exact words of Milt Minsky at the morning coffee clique over at Nickano's Downtown Diner on Platte Avenue between 13th and 14th Streets.

"Did you say 'no small hay'?" asks Kenny Smold, and there's the right side of Kenny's mustache curling up as mocking as a crow on a cow barn.

"You bet your sweet bippy, I did," says Milt like he's swearing out a warrant for shoplifting. Milt, who owns the hardware store, the dress shop, and the Tivoli Movie Theatre, never missed an episode of *Laugh-In*, back in the day. Ol Milt he's dunkin his sticky bearclaw in his coffee, which, as the senior member of the clique, he's been doin for 34 years. Independent insurance agent Kenny Smold, on the other hand, is all about tryin new things, like them zucchini-avocado muffins and carob-mint scones that Nickano, Jr. has added to the yum yums in his bakery case.

"Well, potentially, Euphemion Packing could be the biggest employer

in town, you know, and we could certainly use a shot in the arm, job-wise."
Bill McCarmady, president of the Outstate State Bank, has the *Caterwauler*
open on the table and is running a thick finger down Janet's Monday morning editorial as he speaks. "To her credit, she does mention that up front."

"I don't know, Bill," sighs Ray Stidwell of Ray's Fine Furniture, "our
trees are what make our town unique. You know how nice and beautiful
it is down there by the river." With a far off look of woe on his long
face, Ray gnaws at his right pinkie finger, tryin to dislodge a small sliver of
oakwood from his skin, which is calloused from sleepless nights spent in his
garage refurnishing finiture. Uh, refinishing furniture. Ray's got whatchacall
overactive brain activity, mostly in the brain. Last night he finished one hour
of genuine sleep and six genuine wood chairs.

"You're right, Ray." Milt's tryin to spoon a soggy bear-toe out of
his cup, but the dang thing's alive, it's that slippery. "But that's the only
city parcel that's not near residential. And nobody wants to live next to a
slaughterhouse."

"Meatpacking plant," Bill corrects.

"Okay. Meatpacking plant. Same difference."

"Yeah, okay, well even if we disregard the old cottonwoods," says Ray,
sitting up straighter and swirling the last ounce of coffee around in his shiny
cup, "do you really wanna see Cottonwood become another Riverside or
Concord? Those towns are full of illegal factory workers, man. They've got
drunk drivers all over the place, a lot of—you call that half a cup? S'more
like it—they've got, gee whiz, all kinds of criminal activity, even street gangs.
You've read about it. Their schools are overcrowded, their E.R.'s are full.
Some of their neighborhoods are getting run-down and folks that can afford
it are moving outa town. Whadda we need that for?"

"Economic growth, man," says Kenny, and I never could tell if Kenny's
being sarcastic or not. "How do you argue with that great American ethic?"
For a moment or so, a rare thing happens. The morning coffee clique at
Nickano's is so silent you can almost hear the pita dough rising in the back.
Well—that's assuming that pita dough in fact rises.

So, which one a them four coffee-swilling philosophers went and
sprung for this morning's *Caterwauler*? Not a one. Never need to, the
paper's just sittin there snug every morning, awaitin that unicameral conven-
tion of thinkers. Each a which knows full well, but never lets on, that the

slender Publisher herself is their own personal paperboy. Every morning, you see, on her early jog to the office Journalist Janet stops and plunks her own once-read copy of the *Caterwauler* into the first booth on the right at Nickano's, and takes her coffee to go. The thin but weighty journal sits there like a scared rabbit til pert'ner 9:30, when them four dogmatic doughnut hounds start showin up.

By that time, while the citizens of Cottonwood, Nebraska are still digesting this mornin's editorial, Janet is already up in her corner office overlooking the main intersection in town (corner of Platte and Cottonwood Way) settin her sights on the *Caterwauler's* next volley against the meatpacking proposal. She's got that Omaha conglomerate in the cross-hairs.

Her long unpainted fingertips perch themselves on her keyboard like jaybirds ready to squawk. She stares down at her editorial template. She frowns, and you don't ever wanna see a frown like that at this hour of the mornin. "When a city loses its moral compass," swoop her fingers, finally, with some caution, "to the point of destroying its very namesake, its oldest citizen—" And this is where her frown hardens and her fingers start hopscotching all over them keys. Strong words like "greed" and "self-mutilation" start showin up on Janet's computer screen. "If this were McKinley, Alaska, would we level the Mountain to make room for a Wal-Mart?" Her blue eyes has taken on a gleam that reminds you of the feller in that old flick who's stompin on the white knuckles of the other feller who's hanging off the side of that building. Anyways, pretty soon the Editor-in-Chief's pounding her laptop *fortissimo* like a Liberace, only she ain't as dainty as Liberace. "Every big city problem you can think of," she types at the end of the second paragraph, "will soon settle in Cottonwood—without bringing along any of the resources that big cities have."

Comes a knock on Janet's door. "What!!" I gotta take my hat off to ol Galen Nicolette, the advertising sales rep who sticks his brave young head in that doorway.

"Hey Janet," says he while he coaxes the rest of hisself into that hallowed office. "Can I offer a twenty-five per cent discount to John Cox for his regular ad?" Galen's referrin to the owner of the Happy Strikes Bowl and Brew, up north of town. "Because he doesn't wanna renew, he doesn't see enough business from it lately." Galen's kinda smiling at his boss, but it's the smile of a man whose head hurts.

She says no awful quick, and unfortunately she puts a pretty strong word before the no. "They can go bury themselves, for all I care."

But Galen's a gutsy feller. He rests one paw on the dusty glass case of golf trophies next to the shredder. Galen points out that there ain't no other advertiser to fill up that half page, especially on short notice.

"Who needs them?" says the boss lady, in a voice that could give hate a bad name. "Their ambiance stinks anyway. Their beer, I'd rather drink floor wax." I don't think any recognizable words come outa the young man's throat before he retreats through that doorway and closes it tight, probly wishing he had one of them beers right about now.

Which leaves her back to glaring at her computer screen, and I think I heard somethin like "chhhhe" come out of her gloomy mouth. Anyways, it's a good thing when she's workin in the office nobody can see or hear Janet Hinderson cept a horde of pictures on the wall. Some are black'n white, some are color, but all of em are pictures of a feller having his picture took with other folks. Some of em the feller's young, some of em he ain't so young, but all of em he's got a crew cut and he's wearin a short-sleeved dress shirt and tie. Cept the ones where he's playin golf. The other folks in the pictures—well, you might recognize a governor or two, a coupla writers, a coupla ballplayers. Oh, the wall's got some other things besides: some framed headlines and editorials, some kind words of appreciation on wooden plaques—nice swanky wood, not like these cheap walls which are fake wood paneled.

Best thing about the office, if you ask me, is the big picture window overlookin the street, which ain't all that clean. I mean the window, not the street. The street's mighty clean, fact the whole town of Cottonwood is clean as a bell, like all these little Nebraska towns. If Janet was of a mind, she could look out and see pert'ner the whole town from here. There's the post office across the street, which besides the *Caterwauler* building itself and some of them downtown storefronts, is the only one of the classy old buildings left standing. Over across U.S. Highway 30 there (we call it Cottonwood Way goin through town), you can get an eyeful of the BigMart discount store, on the exact spot where the old Cottonwood Palace Hotel was tore down in '63. That hotel was as pretty a thing of red and white bricks and arches and gables as ever you did see. In its last days it was kind of a old folks residence, with its age-old lobby of walnut and mahogany kind of a meetin place for anyone who liked books, paintin, stamp collectin, or just passin the time. Last one to get kicked out fore they tore her down was old Mrs. Van Druten, the piano teacher. Weren't for her, I don't suppose no kids in Cottonwood coulda played so much as "Chopsticks."

Look out Janet's window westward down Cottonwood Way, you're sure to notice the Japanese Dealership Mall, with new and used cars lined up and sparklin, day or night, for almost a full block. Yup, you recollect right: that's where Meadowlark Classic Books and Music sat, once upon a time, in the old Hobart Mansion. With nothin else, just trees around it. It got tore down too. Sometimes I almost forgit the way it was.

Look a little further and you got Tacky Taco, Bargain Burger, and all those other joints you see poppin up everywhere. You can't see it from here, but down south on 6th and Platte stands the new City-County Center, where the old courthouse was. The old Courthouse was brown bricks, wide steps goin up to the portico, a bronze dome and spire on top, murals inside, and the cedarwood courtroom that softened the gavel raps of even the meanest judge. The new City-County Center is concrete painted peach, with a X-ray machine to get in.

Well, if you had X-ray vision, you could see right into the Cottonwood County sheriff's department on the first floor of the City-County Center. And being it's Monday morning you'd be right on time for the weekly crime briefing. Crime in Cottonwood County ain't quite up to the level of daily briefings. Weekly'll do.

If you're thinkin about having a sheriff with a nervous condition, Cottonwood County is probably as good a place as any. And most folks figure that's what Sheriff Wendy Healy has: one of them syndromes? You know, one of them kind of heartbreakin deals that brings on sudden head jerks, nose twitches, eye blinks, or maybe blurted-out cuss words. In Sheriff Healy's case, the condition takes the form of mangled words, especially when she gets riled up. But I wanna let you in on the deep dark truth: it ain't no syndrome. Sheriff Wendy Healy ain't from around here. She's all the way from Brooklyn, New York, fifth generation. After high school and two years Brooklyn College, Wendy went in the army and wound up at Fort Riley, Kansas. She liked the open spaces and easygoin folks so much, she never left the plains. After the army she got hired as a sheriff's deputy for Cottonwood County, and pretty soon got elected sheriff. She was a natural. But, somewheres along the way Wendy Healy had got the idea that her normal speech, which sounded a little like Al Capone after a root canal, kept her as something of an outsider with the Kansas and Nebraska folk. So she went and got some of them speech lessons that's supposed to make you lose your accent. The thing is, the lessons only did about ninety-nine point five percent of the job. Which is where the alleged syndrome comes in.

"Okay," announces Sheriff Wendy Healy in perfect diction, as she lays out the usual platter of New York style bagels and cream cheese on the large oak conference table of the briefing room. Why she lugs bagels and not doughnuts when she's trying to fit in with a bunch of small town cops is a mystery in itself. I guess she don't get the connection. "Let's get started. What happened out there on State Route Twelve last week? Why are we missing these thefts of northbound highway mile markers until they're cold cases and we have zero leads? Why is mile marker nine at Pond Lake the last one standing until you get to mile marker sixteen at Norbert? What could we be doing better? Smarter?"

"Um, how about authorizing a little more overtime, Chief?" says a scrawny hawkeyed deputy who's the first to attack the platter and fingers just about every bagel on it before he finally picks whole rye with carraway seeds.

"Not in the budget, Gillespie. And how many times do I have to tell you don't call me Chief."

"Sheriff," commences a young blond-haired deputy roughly the size of Wichita, "I hope I speak for all of us when I say that while we're out there patrolling in God's country, we need to do a little more praying, and a little less playing." Judging by nine sets of darting eyes, the entire police force of Cottonwood County just went on high alert, anticipating trouble.

Sheriff don't look any too tickled at the remark, and she's the one that recruited the erstwhile linebacker from her beloved K-State Wildcats. She pats her short dark curls, which still smell like Tracy Ann's Hair and Nail Salon. "Let's not deviate from the agenda, boys, we've got plenty of—"

"I saw you roll your eyes, Anderson," snarls the oversized Wildcat to a balding deputy at the west end of the table, "you damn atheist, you."

"Shut up, Banacek, you crazy bible thumper."

"That's enough now," hollers the sheriff, and her grim mouth suddenly twists spastic-like around her teeth and fleshy gums. "Either yooz guys shuts your traps, or it's coitains for da bote a yuz!" She stops and freezes, big-eyed and blinkin, like she's just been dashed with a cold pail of water. All the guys take on a sheepish aspect and settle down nice'n meek. So she primly picks up her agenda and they move on to other business: vandalisms, teenage drag racing, GTA's, they size em all up and strategize real professional for about fifteen minutes.

"Okay, listen up," says Sheriff Healy with a sour smack from a large sip of grapefruit juice. "Something a little bigger on the horizon." Smack. "We've been invited—and it's a testament to the quality police work that you men do every day—to partner in a sting operation with Riverside P.D. aimed at trying to locate and bust a meth lab that they believe is operating somewhere in rural Riverside or Cottonwood Counties. They suspect that certain rogue workers from the Euphemion slaughterhouse in Riverside have gone into business for themselves, making medium-grade meth at some well-hidden spot. What I'm looking for at this time are two volunteers to participate in the sting operation—", and no sooner has the word "volunteers" left the sheriff's pink lips than eight unanimous hands go up like rockets from that bunch of roused-up deputies, almost choking on their last bites of bagel and wiping cream cheese from their mustaches. You'd think they was on meth themselves by the fiery look in their eyes. And that's where emotion again gets the better of Sheriff Healy. She blinks at that show of hands and it's like she's lookin at the very ending of *It's a Wonderful Life* for the eighteenth time. "That's what I'm talking about," she swallows. "You boys. Around heah we got nuttin but clee-ass up da wazoo!"

Well, Janet don't give a hoot for the view out her office window, she's obsessed with that there editorial she's hammering. But you and me can shimmy up closer to the big window and look out beyond the main streets. Well, jever see a prettier picture of big old houses on wide shady lanes? How about them not-so-old homes farther out that are more ranch-style, and the shade ain't totally growed yet. Then ya got your newer tract homes. A coupla mobile home parks. Schools, hospital, the public library. Grain elevators? Naturally, down by the U.P. railroad tracks. Agribusiness is King, you better believe it. From this big window you're lookin at a green speckled community laid out all nice'n neat, with all the ones runnin east to west numbered as streets and them that go north and south are the avenues. Only place you might notice anything off-kilter is them few ritzy streets like Ridgecrest Drive that curves around out by the country club.

What's more, Cottonwood ain't so big but what you can't see some of the countryside from a third-story window. It ain't easy to tell from here, but the north end of town does rise up gentle, to a grassy plateau of farmland

and ranches. After that the sandhills. South of town, a course, the mighty Platte River. Aw, I'm joshin you—the only thing mighty about the Platte is it's mighty pretty. Outside of Spring, you can wade across her and barely get your knees wet. Full of sand bars and wetlands. And fringed with cottonwoods, like date palms on the Nile. Including Old Grateful and her hangers-on. Oh, the other cottonwoods around'er are a batch of beauties all right, like Cleopatra's handmaids. But Old Grateful: she's the Queen of the Nile. Aw, an old-timer like me don't have the words. But take one look at her gorgeous trunk, and her wavin arms full of the shiniest leaves anywhere stretchin skyhigh—and you'd run outa words just as fast. See if you don't.

By close around 11:30 Janet finishes her coffee and also the rough draft of her editorial for Tuesday's *Cat*. And she looks kinda proud when she re-reads the thing and then she looks almost like a excited school kid when she reads over the last part which she put down in bold letters, where she announces two contests dedicated to Old Grateful and her posse: a photo contest open to all ages, and a essay contest for eighteen and under. The snapshot and the essay which best portray the beauty and greatness of the old cottonwoods will both get published in Saturday's edition.

"Roger," she says, when she calls down to the city desk, "I want two columns on tomorrow's front page for a special announcement. It'll be in your inbox in thirty seconds. Let me see the final layout ASAP."

Independent insurance agent of the year for Central Nebraska ain't nothin to scoff at. Looks good up on the wall over your big ebonywood desk. Especially two years running. Uh-huh. The only thing is, though, is that if them two years was 2001-2002, and you ain't been in the top ten for the last five years—well, now that don't mean you can't make a decent living. Now does it? And keep a calm good-humored outlook on things?

Well I don't know, but maybe you could imagine there's this practical joker who's gone and tied a little invisible thread to the right corner of Kenny Smold's black mustache and, just for kicks, is yanking it upwards every eight or ten seconds. Could be the three cups of coffee, I don't know. Or could just be the way Kenny's strung lately. The gal at the other end of the telephone line don't know the first thing about Kenny's mustache, or the striped silk tie he's wearing, or his slick ultra modern office suite next to the bank on First Avenue in downtown Cottonwood, Nebraska where he sits giving her the third degree. The only thing she probably knows, I'm guessin, is that she don't like the direction this phone conversation has took, and she's fourteen minutes into her lunch break, and it's starting to drizzle in suburban Peoria.

"I've already spoken to Jack Margolick, Amy." The way Kenny's hunched over his desk, you can see from the light of his computer monitor how kinda thin his hair is getting on the top. "I told you, he's the one that referred me to you. I don't appreciate being run around in circles, Amy." The telephone receiver has formed a stationary bridge between his left ear and his twitching mouth. Out the big spotless window behind Kenny two scraggle-haired skateboarders are eyeing that long handrail up the ramp to the back entrance of the bank. The drive-up teller is rapping something furious on her window but that's thick plexiglass, I doubt if any sound gets through.

"Well, as I said, there's nothing more I can do. Your wife's pre-existing condition makes her uninsurable. If anyone should understand underwriting, it's you, Mr. Smold."

"I've been selling your goddam policies for ten years, Amy. Do you know how much money you people have made off the, the—"

"The company made. I'm on a salary, Mr. Smold."

"And a big fat bonus!"

"It's nothing personal, Mr. Smold, and I'm sorry you're taking it that way. As an independent agent you don't qualify for our group plan, you know that. You and your wife's application is treated like any other individual applicant. You might try Schenectady Mutual, I think their underwriting may be a little more liberal than ours."

"Yeah, they're the ones who cancelled our goddam coverage, Amy, claiming that my wife's condition was pre-existing!"

"Well—"

The colorful words that travel to Peoria and the ones that stay and echo in Kenny's office after he slams the receiver is pretty much the same variety of words, I would have to say, and not the kind that I care to repeat. Anyways, that right mustache is bopping skyward to beat the band when his secretary buzzes him. "Kenny, Mrs. Overton is here. She wants to talk to you about converting her whole life to term life."

"Oh sure," says the Independent Agent, ripping his Peoria Life mouse pad to shreds, "like that's gonna happen. I'll cut my own throat before I convert any goddam policy."

I know that 8-tracks went out with straight hair, but Janet's settin home on her couch tonight, listening to Lionel Richie on her 8-track, which still plays but every once in a while sounds like a space ship landing. She's got her ratty pooch named Scoop to keep her and her tea company. If an ancient dog's gentle snore can be called company. Then she's got a stack of her old high school newspapers the *Cottonwood High Flutter*, and *The Daily Nebraskan* from college, and she was of course the senior editor of both. That looks like the year-end edition from college on her lap, with a wide picture of the entire staff against the wall of the newsroom. It's funny, don't ya think, that she was the editor of the paper and here she's the only one not lookin at the camera when the picture was took. Must a been distracted at the last second, you know how that goes. Ain't nothing over thataways cept the gangly fella standing next of her with the deep eyes and serious beard.

Maybe it's the yellow lamplight, I don't know. But in her pink satiny robe from high school and her legs cocked sidewise on the couch, you can't hardly tell if this is now or way back then. She's took her contact lenses off and her old round specs is sliding down her little sniffly nose like she was eight again and tucked in bed with her big storybook. Her eyes has such a castaway look they could be anywhere. It's a fact, Lionel Richie has the same dang effect on me.

I guess when Janet gets to lookin through her old treasures after a hard day at work, she don't much care how cold her tea turns. Scoop's asleep at her feet, he don't know that time is driftin by.

White shiny wisps, scores of em. Snowing gently down upon the peaceful teepee village by the dabbling creek. Quite fetching, ain't it? Snow is a lovely thing, all the poets say so. Only this ain't snow. Oh, along after midnight you still might feel a pretty sharp chill in these parts even now in late spring. But this ain't no freezin weather, and what's snowing down in the night is the cottony fluff of the cottonwood seeds. Them cottonwoods fling their seeds out in the breeze like confetti on Broadway. The seeds'll drift near or far until they decide to stick somewheres. And if they stick somewheres with good soil and water, they got a fightin chance.

Lark Laying Eggs turns in early, but she don't really sleep to speak of. She lays still with her head on her pillow of doeskin stuffed with deer hair, waitin and watchin the rest of the slumbering clan spaced around the teepee wall swathed in their buffalo robes. Lark is layin there in the wee hours staring upwards into the tented shadows when she sees, floatin down through the air vent at the top, one of them cottonwood seeds. By the low firelight she watches fascinated as the little cottony parachute settles down into the embers and then suddenly spurts upwards on a wave of heat. It glides about for a second and then descends toward the gaping cavern that is the mouth of Lark's pop, Eats No Breakfast, who ain't breathin whatsoever. All at once he snorts in a huge gulp of air pulling the bit of fluff halfway down his windpipe, then just as suddenly expels a giant gust which sends the charmed seedlet back up into the stratosphere, so to speak, of the teepee. Well, it spirals down and hovers a bit above the peaceful head of her young cousin who's visiting from the Hunkpapa Sioux up north. Some airy whisper puffs it gently toward her sis, who's lying back to back with a big hairy dog named Scout. Running Water's doing some shuddering in her sleep, having one of them disturbing dreams, I would venture. Her hand starts batting in the air—must be flies in that there dream—and she bats the little filament, which soars over Lark's face, takes a spin around the plump pretty cheek of her mom, who sighs in her sleep, and finally wafts down between Lark's wide eyes, which cross for a second, and lights on the tip of her over-complacent nose.

She sits up straight as a shot, flicks the tiny cottony vagabond into the fire, and gingerly crawls out of her bedroll. Throwing a buckskin blanket over her shoulders and clutching a big stuffed satchel, she touches the sacred bundle hanging on the lodgepole above her pop's head. She puts her hand to her heart, then tiptoes out the teepee flap.

Now, things is quite laid back among the Oglala, as you might of already figured out. Rules is few, personal freedom is the norm and folks can pretty much wander where and when they want. But by the way Lark creeps among the still teepees and keeps lookin around her every direction, you kinda get the feeling she'd just as soon not have company at the moment. Just as she's passing by the second teepee on the left, the flap opens and old Pale Dove sticks her wrinkled face out and tosses the contents of a big clay pot sideways toward her next door neighbor. Fortunately, Lark sidesteps and dodges the glop, which appears to be remains of the nightly stew of roast elk and prairie turnips, with boiled dog thrown in as a filler. Fortunately again, Pale Dove is stone blind, so Lark continues on her way with the old wife none the wiser.

Making a left turn, Lark exits the teepee circle and heads for the creek. As she steps from the shadows of the teepees onto the grassy downward path she stops dead in her tracks: coming straight at her and showing not a trace of recognition is a giant human. She stares the huge feller in the eye and then she begins to smile. Back into the shadows Lark softly steps, and the village Contrary with his fake face heading west and his real face blinking at an upside down east, stalks by on his hands. With no inkling that he and a malcontented maiden just crossed paths.

And toward the trickling creek the maiden creeps, her black hair shining in the moonlight, til a dark cloud passes over. Right on cue, a westerly wind stirs up and shakes loose a flurry of cottonwood seeds to fly and chase after the hasty young runaway.

Tuesday

Tuesday morning after dropping her *Caterwauler* off at Nickano's and scooping up her coffee-to-go, Janet jogs across the street and turns into Flo's Family Shoe Store. The store's got one of them front doors with bells that jingle whenever it opens or shuts. Florene, she's probly the calmest easygoingest person you'd ever meet. I'm not even one hundred percent sure she's got face muscles that work. That's how rare it is to see any emotion on Florene. Right now she's running a feather duster over her display shoes along the walls. Janet catches her cradling a beige dress pump in her left hand like she's fixing to wipe the pablum from its chin.

"Morning, Florene." Not breathing hard just deep and thoughtful she lets herself roost upon the first fitting stool she meets.

"Hey Janet," says Florene in a voice in harmony with her face, "did you hear that Candy Swoboda is pregnant with twins?"

"You're kidding, she's my age."

"Well, here she thought she couldn't get pregnant at all, and now she's having twins."

"Good for her."

"And you know Randy Jansen. Tom Sizemore's son-in-law with the sort of hunchback?"

Janet nods just enough to show she ain't clueless.

"Well, he got fired from Albrecht's yesterday." Somebody has went and mismated a couple pairs of men's sneakers on Florene's display. She rights that terrible wrong with little fanfare.

"How'd he manage that?"

"Just guess. They caught him having hankie-pankie with some woman in the dressing room in their Lady's sportswear department."

"Who was the woman?"

"Don't know yet. I'll have to swing by at lunch and see what Esther in their shoe department has to say."

"Keep me posted." Janet picks a Brannock foot measure up off the carpet and starts flipping the width indicator back and forth, back and forth. That might get on my nerves pretty quick, but Florene just gazes down at her as she tickles a whole row of kid's sandals with two or three sweeps of her duster. "Florene, you know that job as gossip columnist is there for you anytime you want it."

"Oh, honey, I don't go in for gossip. I just like to keep up on things. Oh, one more thing, and you might be interested in this: some guy rode into town yesterday in a limousine and checked in at the Best Midwestern. Him and his black driver. Albert the night manager told Lydia from housekeeping—she's my across-the-street neighbor—that the guy is some honcho from whats-its-name meat company. You know, the company that the *Caterwauler*'s been saying wants to put a packing plant here?"

Well, if you'd a guessed that the newspaper gal might resort to profanity at such a moment, then your instincts is good and you win a free facial at the Cinderella Spa and Salon. Did you also foresee her grabbing a work boot off a display by its steel-toe and banging its heel down on the rubber ramp of the fitting stool like she's cracking the world's hardest walnut? Florene just nods slightly and stares at the outburst. She twirls her feather duster. Janet simmers down quick, glances up and wonders if anybody got the guy's name.

Florene says Lydia didn't get the name. "But he wears an eye patch, a fancy cowboy hat, and boots that sound like Tony Llamas."

"Well—he shouldn't be too hard to track down. Thanks, Florene. I better scoot, I'll see you later."

"Bye sweetie. I'll call you as soon as that new running shoe comes in."

Janet gives her a thumbs up and is out the door with such force that even Florene jumps at the ferocious jingling of the bells.

Even before she hits the shower in her office—meanin she's sweaty as a outlaw's horse—Janet ropes in every darn reporter and editor on the staff and shoos em to the four corners of Cottonwood to try to track down that one-eyed beef honcho. Them reporters don't hafta ask what for: they know she wants em to corner that rascal and grill him good. When Ms. Hinderson assigns you an interview, she wants you houndin that varmint til he spills his guts to the world. So her people scatter to all the likely places: the Best Midwestern, of course, Nickano's where he'd smell the freshest coffee and yum yums in town, city hall maybe, Walter's gas station and garage and auto detail. And anywheres else they could think of along the way. Meanwhile Janet skedaddles herself down to Old Grateful to see if maybe the dude come down there to look over the property. Florene stands out in front of her display windows with her feather duster and watches the unusual amount of traffic emanating from the *Caterwauler* building up the street.

There's a good wind blowin outa the west, off the sandhills. I told you how the cottonwoods, with their ten thousand silvery leaves like sails, how they catch the least little breeze and wave and flicker like—well you remember them 1920s flappers in their shimmy dresses? I remember this one gal, oh my, she had the sweetest smile and a pair of—Huh? What in the deuce was I—? You got me off track, buster, I was talkin about somethin. Well sure, I was talking about Janet and how she looks awful small by the side of Old Grateful. And no mysterious strangers around.

She's havin it out with a red squirrel settin on one of O.G.'s lower branches. I think he maybe just pelted her with seeds from his little jabbering mouth. "You little weasel," she says, shakin her fist at him like he's some high-placed news source that just clammed up. Then she throws a look of scorn at Old Grateful herself, who's standing there minding her own business. "You better appreciate what we're doing for you, you overgrown fencepost."

Well, one by one each of her reporters strike out and check in with her on her cell phone. "Come on back," she barks at em, or tells em get to work on that piece about the new sewer line at the National Guard Armory, or some such breaking news item.

Her cell phone rings again, and she swears like it's something crawlin up her leg. "He's where?" she hoots. "What in the—grab him by the belt buckle and hog-tie him if you have to, I'm coming." She floors it back to the *Cat*, running two red lights and the town's got but four to its name. Lord help us. And the stars must a been aligned that all the sheriff's deputies was occupied elsewhere. Into her parking space plows the publisher, and through the city room she thunders. "Why'nt ya call me?"

"We did—" says poor Beverly, almost choking mid-chew, to the rush of overheated air that lingers in the wake.

In her windblown hair and sweaty T-shirt declarin "Journalists Do

It On Deadline", the *Caterwauler's* chief comes out to the front desk and sure enough there's a lanky one-eyed gent just the way Florene described'm. Except his fancy cowboy hat is sittin on one of the visitor chairs next to his briefcase. Something about this feller's face, though, don't go with the cowboy look. But if you was a mite nearsighted and you was squintin, you may just think you was looking at—well, you know that grinnin cowpoke that you used to see on the TV whose name is on the tip of my durned tongue. Hang it all! Oh, one more thing: the eyepatch ain't black like you think of pirates and all. This here eyepatch is plush and it's crimson red, the color of—well you just never mind what it's the color of.

Now, when it comes to faces, Janet's own has changed mighty fast in three seconds gone by and now she's as calm and self-assured as a corporate veep. "Morning," says she. "What can we do for you?" Beverly the reception-ist is peekin through the doorway with her mouth open. She's got crumbs from her apricot danish still stuck there. More on her dress, but they kinda go with the pattern.

"Good morning." I can't make out the grin on this feller's face, but there's something kinda peculiar. "We'd like to take out a full-page ad for the rest of the week. My company has sketched a layout here." He's got a manila folder in his hand. The ring finger's got a right swanky fraternity ring of some sort. James Garner: that's the name I was tryin to get at.

She sticks out her hand, and boy, ain't she the cool cat. "Janet Hinderson, publisher, I run this poor excuse for a newspaper." She gives a itty bitty bow of the head, and flaps her other hand at her sweaty duds. "I apologize, my personal trainer just left."

"Steve Cosetti," says the guy while he's shakin her hand and eying her like he don't quite know what to make of her. He pulls out a business card from the little lapel pocket on his eyetalian suit and hands it to her. She always was a fast reader, and the only thing on the card that might of threw her was the "General Counsel" part. That probably explains her little dusty eyebrows goin up for a mere second.

"So what's the, uh, nature of this ad you want to place?" and she ain't smiling back as she bobs her head toward the manila folder and fixes her blue high-beams on the feller.

"Basically, my company wants to meet the people of Cottonwood so we're throwing a barbeque on Saturday, hoping that everyone in town will show up."

Her features has slightly froze up, only the eyes is blinking like they can't quite figure the proper focus. She starts to nod. "Fine," she says, "but we want an interview."

"You want an interview."

"An exclusive, obviously. Just a little article about your company and its, oh, long-term plans."

"Mmmh." His voice just got way deeper at the same exact second that his grin shrunk away. "No interview, no ad is I guess what you're saying."

I wouldn't say that a bunched lip is Janet's best look. "We're all about the *quid pro quo* here, as the saying goes." She glances at his card again and flings it on the counter like a discard in gin rummy.

His black eyebrows (the left of which is just stickin out from the patch) is doing the stuff that eyebrows do when there's seismic activity epicentered in the brain. There's another fella, now, come up to the *Cat's* big front window, shading his eyes with a huge hand, trying to see in through the tinted glass. Maybe you used to read the sports page once in a while. That's right—that there is Laertes Norris, the ex-Husker. Second string All Big 12 wide receiver? Didn't quite make the pro draft, you recall. Looks quite different in a white shirt and tie, though don't he? Seems to be waitin on this fella Cosetti.

Speaking a which, he finally goes and agrees to be interviewed and says he'll be back at noon with his limo to take her for lunch. Who has the best chicken fried steak in town he wants to know. From the inside doorway Beverly the receptionist straightens up and raises a hand. "Treadway's Truck Stop." I think one of those crumbs just got spit out into the air and I think she knows it.

Cosetti and his one eye look at her funny but says "Good" and to Janet says he'll see her then. With his hat and briefcase, he's out the door grinning. Now she grins herself.

"You won't see me," mumbles Janet makin the grin turn snotty. "Beverly, get Rossiter in here, tell her she's having lunch with an exclusive. I got a newspaper to run."

After lunch Tanya Portillo has a daydreamy look on her rosy face, while she sits in her bedroom paging through a heavy book titled *The Medieval Foundations of Neo-Classical Traditions*. Oh. Cancel that. *The Neo-Classical Foundations of Medieval Traditions*. Better. Her hair is a wave of red gold. You'd think she was one of them saints that give off radiance. Until you notice that the light she's drenched in comes from above, so it must be one of them beams of light sent down special from heaven. And then you figure out that the mysterious light is ricocheted off Tanya's big trophy for First Place, Nebraska History Bee, which this time of day catches the sunlight off the old slippery slide out in the backyard. Which don't seem any the less a miracle, when you think about it.

She picks up her cell phone, dials and, with a fingernail that ain't all that clean, digs a short strand of celery from betwixt her upper right molars. One ring and a idle sleepy voice picks up. Tanya asks Keith to enter the photo contest for the newspaper. He hadn't read about it.

"Whaja do this morning?" he says.

"Oh, just some research. You know."

"Local history?"

"I'm a boring person, what can I say."

"Why don't you take the photos yourself?"

"I can't. I start my internship at city hall at two this afternoon. You're a much better photographer. You'll need your wide-angle lens. And shoot vertical."

"Duh."

"Get the other trees in the left foreground."

"I thought I was the better photographer."

"You know I like that spot. The time we took sack lunches down there and the bees chased us for half a mile?"

"I haven't been able to look at egg salad since then."

"I'm the one you threw up on."

"I don't see you gorging yourself on egg salad."

"Mayonnaise is a fascist plot."

It was luck I gotta say that put the Marble Arch Mobile Home Park at the exact spot where it sits out on East Cottonwood Way, no further from Todd's Liquor Store than old Sid Haabert can fling an empty pint. That way, Sid can get over to Todd's and get back to his little trailer without crossing any streets. Sid ain't wore out the sidewalk yet, but he's workin on it. I didn't say it was good luck.

Tuesday is delivery day for Bigelow's Beer Distributor in the greater Cottonwood area. So while his boss is havin lunch with that reporter, Laertes Norris is in Todd's buyin his *Omaha World-Herald*, his *Wall Street*

Journal and his vitamin drink just as the beer truck is pulling up. The beer distributor guy is having a bit of trouble gettin his truck parked properly considering there ain't usually a limo parked there. And steady Sid is of course happily teetering on the sidewalk and with glazy eyes is wavin the beer truck to keep backing up. Which is when Laertes comes out puttin on his sunglasses and glancing at the news about banks going busted in Ireland and Spain. He looks up and, like a strongside button hook in the fourth quarter, suddenly executes a quick hop and a skip and he's at the wheel of his limo to make room for that poor Bigelow's Beer driver. Only he forgits to signal when he pulls his buggy out onto Cottonwood Way. And sheriff's deputies ain't that busy around here that they can't catch a late-model Lincoln Towncar limousine that commits a major moving violation.

"Oh Shivers," says Laertes, only he picks just a little nastier word to let out when them flashers and police megaphone go off. But he pulls over and eyes his sideview mirror where a slow-moving mass of official neck and torso rolls out of the patrol car and gets bigger and bigger.

"Afternoon, Sir," says the blond monolith. "Let's take a look at your license and registration."

Laertes takes off his sunglasses and squints up in some amazement. He mutters somethin that could be "Aw fumbles" but I suspect a different word was audibled. "Oh no, it ain't," he says and his brow and jaw do what they can to assist, the one reporting denial and the other disbelief. "I thought I recognized that ape-like amble." Claims he thought it was a bad mirage.

"And here I thought it couldn't get any better than Wildcats thirty-one Huskers seventeen," says the oversize deputy lookin down with one of them smiles you gotta go out to the midnight horror picture to see. "Just look what the Good Lord has raised from the dead. What in God's name put you on my beat, loser?"

Laertes sticks his sunglasses back on and shakes his head. "Just my lucky day, flunky. I get to spend it in this one-horse ghost town, and then I get pulled over by the biggest—"

"Say, you might wanna watch your language, Mister Norris. We don't appreciate the use of profanity here. This isn't North Omaha."

"No? I coulda sworn." Laertes decides he would like to know how come the big fella is dressed up like Barney Fife in Mayberry USA.

"Living the dream, hotshot."

"No, you done lived your dream when you broke my damn shoulder,

Banacek. I never did properly thank you. Weren't for you, I'd be playing pro ball and never had the chance to land this cushy gig."

"Oh, no. I never could take credit for something I didn't do. You broke your precious shoulder all by yourself, man."

"You just stick with that alibi, Deputy Dog. Don't never let the truth get in your way."

"You're a riot, Norris. So—how'd you end up driving for rich city slickers?"

"Much as I'd love to stay and chat, Banacek, I got to be someplace. So I'll just—"

"You failed to signal."

"The damn beer truck was—oh come on, now. You're not writin me a ticket!"

"Got to. Haven't met my daily quota of sassy black has-beens."

"Oh, now—"

"Any problem here, Deputy Banacek?" Both fellers look up and there's the sheriff pulled alongside in her unmarked vehicle, gazing at them quite intent. Two school kids caught covering up some kind of mischief is how them two big fellers look at the moment. Sheriff's gazing and Banacek's mumbling some response and Sheriff says she'll take it from here as she locks eyes with Laertes the instant he takes his shades off. He just swallows. Now, you know how sometimes there's one of them cheesy scenes with the lonely gal and the downhearted fella, and the two of em catch sight of each other across some smoky room of noisy people? And how their eyes lock together for the first time like they was magnets? And how they keep inching and winding toward each other and are full in love by the time they get nose to nose and speak their first hellos? Well, this ain't like that at all.

This is more a case of two creatures bumpin snouts over a half-rotten apple, and rubbing their beady eyes. Not sure if one another is fish er fowl. In fact, somethin that sounds like "I'll be a fricken chowdahead" spits out of the sheriff's little mouth as she shifts her unmarked buggy into park without taking her round eyes off the lawbreaker currently under investigation.

"You owe me eight dollars and fifty-eight cents." If I give it any thought, I'd have to say that Peg Rossiter is the only living soul with the guts to talk back to Janet, let alone startle the poor publisher when she's sittin at her desk and checkin herself in her little compact mirror with the crack that looks like the fork between the South Loup and the Middle Loup before they trickle down into the North Loup. Anyways, she's took her shower, I can tell that, and cleaned up good. Now if she'd just do somethin with her—aw, nevermind.

"Go ask Galen for the petty cash box, he was the last—dammit, did the big shot talk or didn't he?"

Rossiter talks worse'n me, but writes like Longfellow and Thoreau put together. "Goose egg, sweetie. Gave me nothin I couldn't a got from the company handout. Didn't apologize, said he was deliberately misled. Why'nt you tell me he was expecting you?"

"Damn. What difference does it make who—. Now I'm going to have to put on a dress and take the bum for dinner. Did he get his chicken fried steak?"

With her thick arrow-straight hair, her buckskin dress, and almost everything she brung with her soaked clean through, Lark Laying Eggs has been threading the weedy shallows of that serpentine creek the whole entire night and now pert'ner the whole day. Every little bit she looks around northward up the creek. Not a human being anywheres. She ain't rested but once or twice, to munch a little pemmican under the vault of some weeping willow. Nothing ain't colder than a cold rain.

She's slowed down, as the day's worn on, shivering and moving stiffer and wearier. I don't care for the sound of that cough. At last she's sloshed to the very junction with the Shell River—her people's name for the Platte—and wades across. Just as she's up on the south bank, panting and wobbly, rain lets up, clouds break for a second, and the sun pours down on a small slice of Sioux Lookout up ahead southeastward. Sioux Lookout: it don't look like much. Just a gentle rocky rise above the Platte River valley. But for yours truly, well—let's say for instance I'm a flat dry buckwheat cake. That's okay, it don't bother me. Then Sioux Lookout is a pretty good lump of buckwheat.

Lark's poor feet, though they was always calloused by nature, are scraped and blistered up pretty bad. She puts on her sodden moccasins and heads for the point that the sun seems to've spotlighted. It's a trifle steep up that rocky north face. Her feet is dragging, her eyelids drooping, but she's wearing a brave smile as she gets higher, drier, and nearer to that sunbathed bluff. Along with the little scrub junipers scattered about, Lark's long damp hair starts to flap in the gusty wind. Wind up here whistles extra shrill, showin off her upper vocal range. The young maiden cuts quite a picture against the rough sky and endless me stretched below: no highways, no cattle feedlots, no neon signs—just little old *moi*.

No more'n twenty feet from the top she stops with a look of puzzlement, then a low indrawn gasp of "Uhh!" At Lark's feet the blunt tailend of a dusty rattlesnake vanishes behind a sunny white rock, and she quick hobbles to the top. She drops upon a flat boulder and yanks her left foot up and sure enough there's red bite marks on her brown ankle and very little color left in her face. For a long moment she winces skyward like she's tryin to make meaningful eye contact with old Sol through the parting clouds. Then she opens up her big satchel and starts to rummage for two or three small pouches. Well, she sprinkles some herbal concoctions—probly old snakeroot, horehound or some such—into a hollowed-out gourd cup. Then, lookin mighty grim but not scared, Lark takes her water bag which was once a buffalo belly and pours some into the mix. After stirring with her middle finger she applies a plaster to the swelling bite, then adds more water and imbibes the rest. She pulls her buckskin blanket over herself, lays down shivering on the flat rock and closes her eyes to the coy Sun that's still in his jammies and only once in a while peekin out through a ragged stormy curtain.

Well, all around the still maiden the wind's awhistling like she couldn't care less: high and sharp, to my ear. Nothing else ain't stirring. Unless you happen to notice some low moans in a minor key, an occasional sigh in a hoarse baritone. Some muffled snickering like a broken fiddle being plucked? The thing I didn't tell you about Sioux Lookout: just that it's haunted.

Late that afternoon Keith calls Tanya. "I know what you did, and it won't work," he says point blank.

"Yes," she says. "It will. Even if it doesn't."

"I shouldn't even be talking to you," His bleached blond hair rustles in the light breeze of his folks' front porch. "You used me. Me and my twenty-eight-two hundred mm telephoto zoom lens."

"You angled like I said?"

"When have I ever not done what you've asked me to?"

"You don't have to send it. Or put my name instead."

"I've never had my name in the newspaper," he says kinda absent-like after moments of dead silence. "Well, except for Drama Club." Keith goes inside his house and sits down at his open laptop. Tanya don't say a word at the other end. Seems like young people got no caution or fear on their computers these days. They'll do stuff and click and send things without a second thought, to that great mailbox in the sky. Keith, he's a high school graduate and all, but that don't mean he ain't still essentially a kid.

She made it plain that he was her guest. "My folks are lifetime members." It ain't the only civic club in town, but the Grouse Club—FOOG, Fraternal Order of the Grouse—is the swankiest. When it comes to décor and high-class service, their dining room has got the others all beat to you-know-what. Well, I guess Janet's charmed herself up to match the place, cause she's carrying on politer and sweeter than I've remarked in quite some time. That blue dress she ain't wore since Florene's youngest daughter's wedding don't look so bad. And her hair ain't so bad, what she done with it, some kind of wave job.

Now here's the sad part. When this fella Steve Cosetti walks into a place, I'd a bet it's the last thing in the world he wants, but all the other folks become one-eyed too. Because—spite of what they know is bad manners—they can't help staring at the guy out the corner of one eye whilst they pretend he ain't there with the other eye. Which is dang close to being one-eyed. Anyways, I guess he's kinda used to it. But tonight he sorta unfortunately draws attention to hisself when he walks in.

"Ahhhh!" he lets out, loud and sharp, when he bumps head-on into a fancy post or pillar by the maitre d' stand (I told you the place was swanky). Yup, the folks is staring. Janet I guess savvies on the spot that havin only one eye to navigate with messes up a feller's depth perception. She takes his arm. Gets him seated. He don't seem to mind. They order drinks and dinner. Milt and Estelle Minsky are sittin at a nearby table finishing up their salads and waitin on their steaks, naturally somewhat curious.

Milt looks over at Janet and Cosetti, then raises his eyebrows at his wife and says "Verrrrrrrry in-ter-est-ing. But vee vill see," like old Arte Johnson on *Laugh-In*. Estelle gives Milt a warning look but, fact is, just about everybody in the club has their eyebrows raised and is whisperin amongst theirselves.

Steve Cosetti holds up the bottle of Platte Valley Edelweiss wine that their waitress just poured from and reads the label. "Mmmh. Wednesday," he announces. "That was a good year."

"Don't be a big city snob, Mr. Cosetti. We're not so backwards. We have indoor plumbing and everything." She picks up her wine glass and drinks pretty deep, for his benefit. The background music from the bar is The Girl From Ipanema, and I can't even begin to recall the last time I mighta saw Janet sway to music and bite her lower lip so fetching. "You know," she finally speaks kinda soapy and syrupy as the song fades out, "Peg Rossiter says you're a walking infomercial. So, what does Euphemion Packing Company want with a little town like Cottonwood?" A half-smile flits about her mouth as she slaps margarine on hot sourdough, and that's half a smile more than you barely ever catch on Janet. But you see how she don't waste too much time cuttin to the chase, regardless.

"The question is, what would Cottonwood like to see from us?"

"Uh-uh."

"Mmmh." With a slow sip of wine but an eye as perky as boiled coffee, he briefly regards the fireplace mantel where two stuffed grouse with spread wings have been glaring at one another since Janet was sitting here swinging her legs and whining for her Kiddie Plate cause I'm so hungry Daddy. "Fair enough," says Cosetti. "What we want, Ms. Hinderson, is to be part of a growing progressive community. We want a partnership in which we give back more than we get."

Her eyes is more amused than her mouth. "That sounds lovely, but lets look at reality. Your plant in Concord was shut down for two months last year due to immigration violations. Twenty-two percent of the total workforce was found to be undocumented. I wrote the article myself. Since the initial opening of your plant, the town of Concord has seen a forty-six percent increase in DUI's and similar increase in traffic accidents. Their school district is now facing—Mister Cosetti, why are you shaking your head?"

It's just that the way he sees it, new growth, new industries, these things involve some adjustments at first. Fact of life. Is she telling him that her readers don't want economic expansion, period? "Should New York and Chicago be dismantled?" he says. "Just because everything isn't perfect and pastoral?" Stuffed grouse can't roll their eyes and make sarcastic faces. Jever dwell on that?

"So you consider crime, public safety, let's see, school overcrowding, neighborhood blight, you consider these issues to be nothing but minor adjustments that the people of Cottonwood should just blindly accept. Teresa, what happened to dressing on the side?" Someone in the kitchen's gonna have to eat that salad.

Sounding good and righteous, he puts up a eloquent protest and says he's bein misjudged by her and that he'd never belittle the honest concerns of her readers. And his company's got strategies, he says. To keep all problems to a minimum. Stuff like housing plans, medical plans, and a new hiring system to make sure only legal residents get put on board.

Janet don't seem impressed with this hombre that can dodge questions about as slick as Frank and Jessie James did the noose. Well, fair's fair and in the limo she was determined to sidestep every which question the poor barrister tried to get out of her: where she'd went to school, how big is her editorial staff, what have you. Can't say as I blame him for—

"And what about the landmark cottonwoods? Which you'd be destroying."

"We think the city council is in the best position to determine what's most beneficial to the community," says he tilting his wine glass like the whole town of Cottonwood sits inside and waits to be rated for clarity and bouquet. "We trust their judgment."

"Mister Cosetti: I assume you're speaking at the council meeting on Monday."

"I am."

"Good," and up she stands. "You've got your script all ready." With her notepad and purse she starts to leave him in the dust, then turns. "We'll run your ad, but that's not all we'll run." As she heads out of the place Janet writes in the air mouthing "tab" to Teresa, who's just now comin out the kitchen with her salad. Teresa ain't the only one with dismay written on her face. Except for Cosetti hisself and his bigheaded grin as he watches her go, seems like everybody in the club lets out a little groan. Milt throws down his napkin in disgust, looks at his wife and sputters out "The Fickle Finger of Fate strikes again, Estelle."

What do you suppose? Could these good folks have been under the mistooken notion that maybe this here dinner with a stranger was some kind of a date type of thing? Was they all chomping their steaks but prayin under their breath, lost in daydreams of Janet in white at the First Methodist Church with her hair done up fancy? Was they all mentally forecasting a tropical storm downgraded to a sweet summer breeze?

Steve Cosetti looks around, unawares and undisturbed, then up and orders a round of drinks for every last disappointed soul at the FOOG.

After sinking all her change (and a swift kick for good measure) into the city room snack machine, Janet settles down to a toothsome dinner of granola bars and Cheeze-bits. Appears like she's already typin up that interview and ruminatin on the best adverbs to describe that cagey meat mogul. Peg Rossiter's brung in coffee from the minimart and she's standing looking over her boss's shoulder. The green linoleum is humming as the presses start to warm up in the basement. It's after nine o'clock and Janet takes a break to check her emails and not twenty seconds later she gets the dangdest look. Consternation don't really describe it so I don't know why I mention that but she yanks Peg by the collar to within four inches of her laptop screen and Rossiter registers something different and similar both that also ain't consternation. She just shrugs at her boss and her boss shrugs at her and they both shrug at the screen which I imagine might cause considerable consternation on the part of that computer.

Then Janet calls all the late editorial staff together, sends em scurrying, pounds her laptop, telephones certain persons and emails others. I don't know, but she might want to go easy on them granola bars next time.

In a nice polo shirt, slacks, and some pretty choice cologne, the ex-Husker is out to snare somebody, that's plain as day. He stops in Cosetti's room to make sure his services ain't needed for the balance of the evening. The general counsel has mysterious documents on his laptop that need poring over I guess with his lawyer's eye. And that eye can't wink but it can grin, once he cracks the door and catches sight of Laertes. "Who, me?" says he settin back down on his bed, "Stand in the way of young romance? Not a chance, hot shot."

"You know it's nothing like that, boss," says the big guy. Pert'ner as humble as when he stood up at the All Big Twelve banquet.

"Hey, Don Juan." Cosetti don't let Laertes get out the door quite that quick. "She gonna cuff you first?"

The big fella grabs the doorway, turns askance at his boss and says "Chhhhe. You're gettin racy in your old age, man." Cosetti just waves him out after cracking something about being careful out there and havin the right to remain silent. We can only assume that Laertes appreciates the slick repartee. You know how them motel doors tend to slam if you let em.

Do I believe the Sioux people's number one Lookout over the Platte

Valley is haunted? Well, can you prove it ain't? Anyway, to them they don't see haunted as necessarily a bad thing. Depending on the particular circumstances that brung them to the top of that chalky rockpile.

See I don't know what invisible forces might be hovering about on this windswept promontory, but I guess the Plains Indian has a sixth sense. They believe pretty intense in the sacredness of nature, since that's what they live and die by. Rocks, clouds, birds—all are alive and holy. I'm kinda partial to nature myself, spose I may of hinted at that once't or twice. So the Indian puts herself in nature's hands, prayin for whatever blessings nature decides is meant to be. And they come up to this here Lookout to meditate cause it's closer to the Stars, which holds up the heavens. It's dark and it's silent, and silence is the dimension for extraordinary things to occur.

Anyhoo—the Sun has sank hours ago behind rolling storm clouds. And the moon has now took his place, splashin pale moonlight on the blanketed statuette that is Lark Laying Eggs. The Sioux maiden lies just as cold and still as the slab of stone she's made her bed. You know, it's times like these I wisht I had the Indian's understanding of things. For oftentimes things just don't make no sense. I wisht I could find a way to fathom all these things that ought not to happen in this world but do happen and by golly did one of her little eyes just twitch or am I seein things myself? Cause I was pretty well given up on—yes siree, them dark eyes is open. And they're tryin to figure out where the heck she is and is it a good place to wake up in or should she start to panic. I kinda get the feeling the gal is hearing stuff—sighs, moans, who knows, things that I cannot distinguish for the life of me—in that chill wind. Lark looks to me like her poor red ears is cocked and she's listening, real keen, to some species of voices in the night. I hope they're friendly voices, that's all.

Scraping, scratching, crunching. Like footsteps on loose pebbles. Hold on a minute. I can hear those sounds myself. And they're emanatin from right over there and I mean right over there. If I ain't seeing somethin real and alive creeping over them rocks towards the young gal, then I'll just shut my mouth from here on. Somethin big. Somethin hairy and four-legged. Somethin with its top half just silhouetted against the eastern Moon.

The closer the sounds the bigger the shadow of that silhouette, and the wider and wilder her eyes. Until that shadow is everywhere. Breathing and bending over her and her long-benumbed throat, them eyes the only thing she can move. Suddenly the thing is on her. I can't look. It's, it's too horrible. The licking, the whining! The whining, the, the licking. More licking. More whining. Some panting. Some panting licks. Some whining pants. A little drool. Well. Well now. Hmmmh. If that don't—

Lark seizes the thing's head. She thrusts that head into a beam of moonlight. "Scout!" Lark's big sweet dog? Trailed her all the way from the village? Why, weak as she is she smiles and throws her arms around the panting whining drooling pooch and cries as she ain't supposed to never do.

Well, atop this lonely outcrop the wolf part of Scout arches his powerful neck and yowls a mournful tune for his beloved human. The woman part of Lark laughs and cries pitiful tears at the same time. And the haunted part of the Wind, well—who knows what prophecies she whispers in the vast invisible night.

Wednesday

"TEEN PHOTOGRAPHER DISCOVERS RARE PAWNEE TREE CARVING?"

*F*ramed perfectly by Bill McCarmady's big stubby thumbs, the *Caterwauler's* front page headline—above a shadowy photo—rattles before the banker's ruddy face as he does a pretty good job looking and sounding like Harry Reasoner reading the ABC nightly news and tryin to ignore Barbara Walters sittin to his left. Ray ain't arrived yet, but Milt and Kenny is each washing down their first yum-yum with their first cup of Nickano's fresh brewed. Bill's oratory is plenty loud enough to be heard over the slurps and gulps.

"It's a fake—one of those mocked up photos that all the kids do now-adays on their computers," says Milt over his cup, dunking and rescuing at the perfect millisecond only to gobble what he just rescued.

"That's ridiculous," Kenny answers back. "The kid isn't that dumb. He knows the tree is sitting right there next to Old Grateful, Milt, and can be checked out in five seconds." Yup, the right corner of Kenny's mustache is sticking up like a black hairy worm poking out of a pale pink apple. "What's fake is the idiotic carving itself. I can tell with one look that the kid carved it himself. It's too, it's too—"

"Yeah but," says Bill, "article says they've already had old E.M. Tinker from the local historical society confirm that the design is consistent with Pawnee artifacts. And the Pawnee Nation has been contacted and their lawyers are expected to be heard from today."

In walks a hangdog Ray Stidwell with his left eye closed, his head tilted right and rubbing the kinks from his neck with a varnishy hand.

"Smile, Ray," says Kenny. "Your precious cottonwoods might be tied up in litigation for years."

"Whatja say?" says Ray like he don't know where he is or how he got there. He sets down and, while they quick fill his cup, they fill him in on the local drama being played out.

Meanwhile Milt's tugged the paper from Bill's grip and he's got it open to the big ad put in by that fella Cosetti. "Say," says Milt, who don't outright drool, normally, but he salivates pretty regular. What kind of dessert, he wonders aloud, might they serve at that barbeque, and is it all-you-can-eat?

Kenny don't even hear Milt behind the newsprint. He's leaning across the table and studyin with calculating eyes that front-page stonewall interview with Cosetti and the honcho's picture next to it grinning wide at the *Cat's* photographer. You know, Kenny's right mustache might get permanently stuck in the upright position if he ain't careful.

About ten in the morning Janet lays the beef baron's card on her desk and calls. "Mr. Cosetti, you may want to get a hold of someone who knows about Indian art."

"Mmmh. I've read your article and my staff is already on it. You shouldn't have published it, you know. It's an obvious hoax."

"We said it's under investigation. That's the truth."

"Ah, freedom of the press." And it's good there's a bunch of cellular airspace between her glare and his grin. "You gotta love the founding fathers."

"Oh I do, Mr. Cosetti. With all my heart."

"I'll tell you who I admire, Ms. Hinderson. There's a wise person who once wrote 'With freedom comes obligation. With freedom of the press comes the obligation to never print what conscience and integrity deplore'."

As sudden as a summer cloudburst, her face and his eyepatch is almost the same red and her breathin gets awful quick. It ain't like Janet to stammer. "Mr. Co—Where did you—"

"I've got to hang up now, Ms. Hinderson. Thanks for the advice." He grins and continues to walk away from a brick building on Avenue A, one block east of Platte Avenue, that says Peters and Brockley, Attorneys at Law. He gets in the limo, Laertes Norris puts down the sports page and drives off. Then the Euphemion general counsel sets back in his Scottish leather interior, monkeys with his phone for a second and opens a little memo. He puts an X next to the very first name, Gus Peters. The memo's got four other names on it.

She's got me all to herself, in a way. I got grasses and greeneries rising up in splendor, I got birds nesting, coyotes half-dozing, ants doubletime marching. But what I ain't got is another human being in sight, and we're talking miles on miles. Lark don't seem to mind the infinite solitude, and in fact she's humming a sweet little tune and bounding eastward cross the plains with Scout rambling at her side. As if bein feverish, snakebit and sleepin on a high cold slab is things that happened to some gal in a near-forgot whimsical fable of long ago.

Now if she's lookin to find the Pawnee people anywheres, Lark's course is right on the nail. Pawnee country's due east and no surer way to find it than simply follow that river and keep it right there in sight over your left shoulder. That's what she's did so far. But so far ain't far enough.

Somethin's amiss, and what's amiss is that Scout has raised his twitching snout to the air, wheeled around, and cocked his ears like antenna. By the time Lark catches on, Scout's got a good mournful howl echoing southwestward toward the low hills and plateau country that they'd already put between them and Sioux Lookout itself. Lark Laying Eggs ain't one to panic, as you know, but dogs don't howl for no reason. Oh there's a little thunder back southwest, but that's about it. One thing wrong with that observation, though: there ain't a cloud anywheres near that part of the sky. Um—well that ain't quite true. Now there is a cloud, but not the kind you look up at and think it looks like Aunt Frieda with two noses and her hair in curlers. This is the kind of cloud that billows straight at you and hits you in the face at thirty, forty miles an hour.

Now buffalo, which you may not believe on account of their massive heads, horns, and shoulders, are actually one of the most nervous and skittish critters on the whole prairie. So much as a sparrow or a leaf in the wind could spook a buffalo and start her bolting across the plains, which means the entire herd—could be thousands—will run blindly after her for dozens of miles at a time. They don't know why, they don't know where: they just do. You don't really want to be in the direct path of a stampede of bison if you can possibly help it. And, whereas I tend to be a bit on the dusty side, you don't even want to be downwind. These noble critters kick up a load of dust.

So happens Lark is both: the critters and their dust cloud is simultaneously stampeding in her direction. Cept the wind musta came up and the dust gets to her first. She starts to cough and choke. No place to run to even if she could run half as fast as that thundering horde. Scout somehow is able to keep up his yowling and yelping as them buffalo grow near. And nearer they do indeed grow.

I can't read the minds of buffalo or any critter, but I suppose if somethin as innocent as a prairie dog could spook em, then a big howling wolfish fella like Scout should send them bison into hysterics. And bless his heart, Scout keeps up such a wail that would raise goosebumps on a corpse and, no more'n a hundred yard off about two-thirds of that herd suddenly veer left (their left) and head down toward the river. They was pretty thirsty anyways, stampeding and all. Well the other third don't seem to realize they been ditched, so they're comin gangbusters. Not thirty yard from Scout's nose, the lead cow all at once digs in her hooves and the remainder smash up behind her, and then they all disintegrate into a mad morass of panic, colliding, goring and finally turning tail in all directions. Scout yowls a while longer, for good measure. And as the dust starts to clear you would guess that right about now Lark is sincerely relieved and giving a prayerful thanks to the Great Spirit for not lettin her be pulverized by about seventy, eighty thousand buffalo hooves. That's a blessing all right but the Great Spirit might have to wait on bein spoke to, since presently the young gal's gone and collapsed unconscious in a patch of new sunflower and clover where the wind sweeps away the chalky dust that coats her pressed lips and deep locked eyelids.

After Janet lost the power of speech, she spent several minutes snortin little breaths out her puzzled nostrils and screwing her eyes up at her cell phone as if that Cosetti dude musta lapsed into Portuguese just before he hanged up on her. All she's done since then is piddle, then she tried some dillydallying, and she even done a fair amount of lollygagging while she was at it. This from a gal who don't never let the grass sleep on the job.

Lunchtime she restlessly looks out her office window, which she never does do by the way, and sees the limo heading straight down Platte Avenue. She mulls for a second then dashes downstairs, I think I mentioned she's a jogger. Jumps in her car and heads down Platte likewise. Parks and walks toward Old Grateful. Sure enough, the limo's parked there too and, on coupla big motel blankets laid out on the soft ground beneath O.G.'s generous arms, there's Cosetti, Laertes and two young gals what look like interns or assistants or some such. The latter young fillies is both talking on their phones and writin notes on pads. Cosetti has papers spread everywhere around him on the blanket—legal materials, looks like, financial records, marketing stats, architect's plans, an Environmental Impact statement or two, and a couple big bills from local caterers. Would you say that maybe this fella Cosetti has too many irons in his plate right now? Well, all the four of these Euphemion folks is eatin giant drippy burritos from Tacky Taco while they work. That is, Laertes ain't workin exactly, he's just readin the police notes in this morning's *Caterwauler*, and kinda lookin around dreamlike at the birds and trees and river easing by. Once in a while a solitary cottonwood seed drifts past searchin for its longgone playmates, and Laertes will swipe at it but misses every time.

There's a tall telescoped ladder fastened against one of O.G.'s lovely sidekicks, and upon the ladder is old E.M. Tinker from the historical society. With palsied hands he's attempting to measure what he referred to in his interview with Rossiter as "a small arborglyph"—fancy word for tree carving—that looks to me like a man-bird riding an arrow. Somethin like that. The old professor's writin measurements and descriptive words in his little notebook, and every once in a while pulling his bifocals off and glancing down with a smile at them two young gals with their legs angled so graceful on them blankets.

It don't take long for Janet to buck up and march down that little woodsy path toward the river, every bit the journalist. Leaves and twigs strewn all about, she can't exactly sneak up on anybody with her crackly footfalls. Seven eyes and one easy grin greet her. "Mr. Cosetti," says she like they'd only pushed the pause button on their earlier conversation, "I somehow didn't peg you as a nature lover. Gee I can't imagine why," and with palms, eyes and mouth all raised in mock wonder she searches the cottonwood firmament as if the clue just might be whispered there.

"Mmmh." Seems like Cosetti's heard that joke before. "Join us, Ms. Hinderson. You know Laertes, and these are my—"

"I wanna know why you memorized something from an editorial I wrote nine years ago and quoted it at me." She folds her arms over her chest and juts a hip. "That strikes me as very strange and I think I'm entitled to an explanation."

He goes and admits the allegation that he's read her editorials but won't say why. "It's not something I can just glibly answer." That don't relieve the wonder in her eyes one jot. But then the dude up and offers "Perhaps over dinner tonight we could—" Sometimes half a shrug is all you got.

Six corporate eyebrows go up, Janet looks believe it or not almost tempted. But when it comes down to it she tells the worthy barrister she's tied up for dinner.

"Mmmh," is how he swallows that particular snub. But his grin wakes up pretty quick and stretches itself with a sniff of utter disinterest. The blue eyes of the press full upon him, the dude throws his last few tortilla chips for the birds and begins studyin an important looking spreadsheet. The only detail I might bother to point out—besides the Wind swooping in and rustling papers and leaves alike—is that the document Cosetti's so absorbed in is upside down.

Well, while Janet troops back to her car, a dark figure hides behind a clump of willows and scans the vicinity like a mud-caked Cherokee scout. Standin there, watching like a hawk, a hungry hawk that ain't caught but a sparrow or two this week. None other than your friendly neighborhood Independent Insurance Agent. I'll be durned if, snazzy pinstripe suit and all, Kenny ain't toting a fishin rod and reel over his shoulder just as casual as if everybody knows that Wednesday afternoons are for playing hooky from the rigors of selling insurance. The instant Janet drives off, Kenny's on the riverbank, fly casting for channel catfish. With every cast, his eyes dart eastward toward them outatowners and he sidles downstream a yard or two. He's soon within earshot, but he's a regular Robinson Crusoe, Kenny is, that hasn't an idea in the world that any other soul could be within five thousand mile of this uncharted wild.

All of a sudden, not but twenty feet away, he looks around him amazed. Why, there's human beings here, lord a mighty! says Kenny's wide brown eyes. Trouble is, nobody on them blankets is particularly interested in eccentric smalltown anglers, and he's just a smudge on the landscape to them busy corporate cogs. Well, Kenny's had to toss his pride away more than once or twice in his professional career. "Oh, almost had im!" shouts Kenny like a stage-actor in a noisy theater, reeling in an empty hook. No one's paying the least attention when he looks around so he just laughs as awkward as that stage-actor's understudy and slogs ahead in his muddy wingtips. Stumbling over gnarly roots and their little sprouted baby O.G.'s, he reaches the edge of one of them blankets. "Afternoon," he says shouldering his fishin rod and eyeing them profit statements down by Cosetti's feet. The folks look up and smile for a short second, then look down and resume their business. No Solicitors Allowed at this here mobile office.

"Say," exclaims Kenny with a snap of his fingers, "didn't I see your picture in this morning's—? You're uh, you're uh. With that big company that's putting a, a—"

Steve finally grins a skeptical grin up at the poor devil and extends a hand. No sooner has the two fellas give out their names than Kenny starts speculatin aloud about the vast insurance needs of a meatpacking plant and how truly necessary it is to have a local insurance agent to stay on top of things and, oh by the way, it's lucky they run into each other because he happens to have a written proposal right here in his suit pocket for comprehensive insurance coverage including fire, flood, general liability, workman's comp, products liability, group medical, group life, group disability, long-term care, group auto and umbrella. Each item seems to pluck at Kenny's right mustache while it drags Cosetti's mouth nearer to the ground.

"Mmmh. I'm sorry Misterrrr—"

"Smold. Kendall Smold, P.I.A., C.F.P."

"Well I'm sorry but my company places all its insurance with our agent in Omaha. You shouldn't have gone to all this—"

"Listen," and Kenny thrusts the proposal like a bayonet into Cosetti's hands, "I can write a fifteen per cent discount into the comprehensive package, I'm willing to do that because—"

Cosetti shakes his head and Kenny pleads with the man to at least take the proposal to their finance department or set up a meeting or something. Well while Kenny buttonholes Cosetti, his forgotten fish line dangles above them young gals who's busy with their executive duties on the other blanket. All of the sudden there's a little cry from the nearest gal, whose hair extension is now hooked and bobbing, fightin for its lustrous blonde life at the end of Kenny's fish line. Kenny and his mustache don't realize he's caught his limit and he's up the creek.

Old E.M. Tinker looks down kinda tickled at the scene below, and Old Grateful looks down with a sad leafy wisdom that you can't get from spreadsheets or software.

Summer is when kids oughta be out and about: baseball, tennis, swimmin at the big Pioneer Park pool up on 8th Avenue. But, on the other hand, if you're more a poet than a pinch hitter, I guess you might spend your lazy June days writin verse. If you're fifteen year old Brandon Sorenson, and you fancy yourself the young bard of Cottonwood, and there's a newspaper essay contest about trees, then there ain't no question but that you're gonna spend one-third of Tuesday and almost half of Wednesday writin the best dang poem you can to send in for that contest. Well, Brandon's done that, and it ain't very long but he saves the final draft and emails it to his mom who's re-readin *Light in the Forest* online out in the kitchen. Well, it don't take long before Mrs. Sorenson, who's the eighth grade English teacher at Cottonwood Middle School, calls out to Brandon that she's read his poem and to please come out to the kitchen. Brandon says okay, and no sooner does he transfer their old cat Miss Havisham from his lap to his bedroom floor and march into the kitchen than his mom smiles and says "Dude," and then "I'm blown away." Which stops Brandon in his tracks and makes him blush that quiet blush that his mom just adores. So a hug from mom which Brandon tolerates for about a second, then he sprints back to his room to email the poem to the *Caterwauler* editor, in plenty of time for the final selection. Good thing the young man can type and click standing up, cause Miss Havisham's in his chair and not inclined to leave her altar anytime soon.

It's a good day to die.
Or it's not.
That's about it right there. That's a pretty good rundown of the plains Indians and their view of things. They sit front row and center on the pageant of life. They see how life and death is sudden and everywhere. If it's meant to be, it'll be. No use buckin the system. That goes for humans, buffalo, dragonflies, or whatnot. Today the buffalo might outrun you. No sweat. Tomorrow the beast will lay down his life for you.

So the roaming village of Chief White Raven of the Arapaho tribe can chew on them deep thoughts if they got nothin else handy to fill their bellies whilst they track the buffalo across the Platte Valley. Or, they can wonder about the young Sioux gal with the long thick hair and what in creation she was doin fainted dead away in the middle of nowheresville. With about eight hundred thousand hoofprints all around. When she comes to—if she comes to, maybe—well, she scared me once before, this time I spose I ought to at least try and embrace the Indian philosophy and see if that don't make me feel a bit less fretful and leave it in the hands of the Great Spirit. That might not do her any harm, and it might just help.

Anyways, Lark ain't dead—that's plain enough, cause her mouth's been movin with some voiceless plea or prayer the last half-mile or so, and now she's startin to groan real low and faint, and little flicks from her tongue come snaking over them parched lips. Two Arapaho gals walk alongside Lark's "sleigh" which is a cottonwood travois, and now the younger of them two goes and sprinkles some tepid water on the girl's lips and brow. The two big harnessed packdogs pulling that travois turn and let out thirsty yowls—they want some of that water too. This all seems to be good medicine, for soon one of Lark's eyelids pries open, then the other, then they unglaze a bit and her inky pupils roll around some and finally lock into position. Then they don't much like what they see. Which is dozens of strange villagers advancing behind her with full camp gear, and the ground weirdly receding away from under her. She would sit up and take stock, I believe, but she can't. Her wrists are snugly lashed above her head to the poles of that travois. The older Arapaho gal chuckles. "Those rawhide bands tighten up nicely," she says in her language, "when they dry in the sun, don't they, Princess?"

Just behind and off to the side, two youthful Arapaho hunters stroll and gaze fondly at Lark as her distress mounts slowly, weak as she is. "Yellow Knife my friend," says the tall long-legged one, "how about a footrace to that old buffalo skeleton at the foot of that knoll. Winner gets the Sioux gal for a wife."

"Nuh-uh!" says Yellow Knife, a husky fella with short legs, as he grasps his heavy bow and quickly draws an arrow from his beaverpelt quiver. "First one to plant an arrow into the left eye of that skeleton from this little sandhill has first dibs on the gal. If she lives."

The two admirers are near about ready to come to blows over how best to settle the right to Lark's hand when they're interrupted by the very voice of their newfound darling rising above their voices and above almost any sound they've ever heard in their brief bucolic lives. Now—whatcha need to remember right here is two things: first thing is that Lark has never sat down and learnt more than a coupla words of Arapaho, and Tricky Spider and Beyond the Tallow Creek ain't especially useful terms in her present situation. Like all plains Indians, she knowed the sign language that tribes communicate with if they don't speak one another's tongue. It's a rough system but it gets the general point across. But you need yer hands to do it. The second fact to keep in mind is that there ain't no swear words whatsoever in the Lakota Sioux tongue. Nor in Arapaho neither. So I guess Lark, finding herself caught in circumstances nigh as galling and absurd as ever she's found herself, she does what she has to do: sets her vocal chords to the highest setting and starts in ad libbing the worst, vilest-sounding made-up words she can produce on the spur of the moment. She makes it mighty clear that she is more than just a little displeased with her treatment and will tolerate it no longer. Struggling with her poor bound wrists, she's carrying on something awful, is Lark Laying Eggs. If the prairies could blush, I'd be red not green. "That's gratitude for you," sneers the older Arapaho gal, who vows that next time they'll just leave the spoiled child sprawled senseless in the middle of nowhere—see how she likes it.

Young Yellow Knife looks just a bit distraught, with his bow and arrow hanging at his side. He finally turns and tells his rival that he's decided to bow out and let go all claim to the maiden's hand.

"No," says Gray Fox, the tall long-leg fella, "she's really more your type afterall, I'll wait for the next one."

"Nuh-uh, you claimed her first," Yellow Knife grouses back.

"Not on your life, chum," yells Gray Fox. "Last one to the river and back has to marry the gal." And off he sprints like the Wind in March.

"You're a low down cheater," hollars Yellow Knife through cupped hands, and he huffs after his diminishing buddy as fast as his stubby legs can churn.

Anyways, Lark pretty soon starts to wear herself out, and some of the Arapaho elders, who trade with Sioux villages all over the plains and know some Lakota, start talkin her lingo and signing as needed and they kinda counsel the unhappy girl not to waste her breath so much with all that screaming and bad medicine. "You keep hollaring like that, young woman," says one of the traders, "and you're liable to start another buffalo stampede."

She gets quiet and subdued for a moment, then she starts lookin left and right sorta frantic and callin out Scout's name. These Arapaho gents seem to savvy that Lark is missing her dog, so they explain that the big fella run off when they tried to put a thong round his neck. Hmmmh. I told ya how the Sioux people don't hardly never cry outside of funerals. Sometimes, though, I spose there can be a funeral taking place right inside your very own heart.

"How many times have you said this to your refrigerator: 'These shelves are too short. I can't fit anything tall in here.'? Sound familiar? Well, now there's an answer. At Wacklund's House n' Home, come see our new line of extra-short disposable food storage bins, designed to fit into even the tiniest refrigerator shelf—"

I just wonder sometimes. It's just a gut feeling and I can't describe it, but is there anything out there that makes a sound half as tinny, or as hollow, or as dang reverberating as a small town a.m. radio station on a Wednesday afternoon in June? One of them days, you know the type. Sultry. Airless, for even the wind blows hot. The entire valley heats up like a oven that pings and echoes as it bakes whatever or whoever is stuck inside with no way out. I guess the radio waves get seared a bit themselves.

"Ridiculous," says Kenny, as he accelerates his snazzy Aculexity SUV west on 21st Street toward home. It's not real clear if Kenny's referring to the radio commercial, the big elm trees all along the street which has just had most of their limbs lopped off by the City, or life in general.

"KOTT weather: continued hot over the next seventy-two hours, lows tonight in the mid-seventies, high tomorrow ninety-four with chance of thundershowers—"

Kenny turns onto Ridgecrest Drive just as Engelbert Humperdinck starts to croon After the Lovin. You know, the one that goes Da Da Dee Dee Dee Dee—. That's the one. He parks in his driveway, wipes a speck of dust off the roof of his SUV, and looks all around the neat cul-de-sac which, but for the West Wind blowin off my Sandhills, would be still as a paintin on the wall. He smoothes the section of his hair that's growed out extra long and blow-dried to cover the bald spot and checks his red brick mailbox at the curb. There's a stack of mail and he shakes his head.

"Hey, guys," calls out Kenny while he locks the front door behind him and looks round for signs of life. There's light playin on the walls of the den so that's where he heads to. There sits Kenny's twin nineteen-month-olds, like bookends, watchin Looney Tunes on the portable DVD player on the floor. And his wife hunched on the couch. "How're my little rugrats?" He's down on one knee, kissing each one on the top of her curly brown head.

"And there's blood," says Liza, pointin at the cartoon antics.

"Then she will die," says Lorna, slapping her chubby little thighs.

Kenny turns a wrinkled forehead to his wife. "Where'd they—"

"It's not the first time you've heard that," says Allie Smold, sipping slowly from a glass of ice water.

"When did I ever—"

"You just don't remember, Kenny. You know your mind is always somewhere else." Did he buy diapers, she asks her husband. He didn't. The cartoons flicker across her ashy face. Didn't he see this morning that they were almost out. She seems bent on knowing.

"Why couldn't you just tell me," says Kenny. "If you wanted to marry a mind reader you should have said something seven and a half years ago. I'd have taken lessons." He snuffs hot air out his nose and bobs his head like there's polka music only he can hear.

He stops and looks at his wife. Her used up mouth. Something washed out in her sore faded eyes. Hung up somewhere far away to dry. Around the dusky room: the designer window blinds pulled down, the swanky recessed lighting turned off. He goes plunks down on the couch and puts his arm around her only not touching just resting on the top of the back cushion. "So when did it start?" and it's rare to hear Kenny's voice so deep and even. Her eyes is staring nowhere, her bare shoulders ticking the smallest of tics. Has she took a Traxamig, Kenny asks. She ain't. "I'll get you one." He gets up and starts toward the bathroom.

"That's gonna be a little bit impossible, Kenny, since we don't have any in the house."

"Whadya mean we don't have any in the house?" he says headin back couchward. "Why don't we, didn't you—" She starts to cry. "Allie! Why haven't you gone and, gone and—"

Which don't help the cryin any, and she flares her wet eyes at him and sputters. "Because it's two hundred thirty-five dollars for ten pills!"

"Since when?"

"When do you think?"

He stares at her like he might cry in a minute himself. "I'm gonna sue Schenectady Mutual, I swear I am. But that's okay, whatever it costs, you need your pills." She don't reply. He'll go pick up a refill after dinner, he says. She's awful quiet all of a sudden. "Okay?"

"With what for money?" finally she says.

He scratches the part of his neck where he shaved too close this morning. "Is the Visa maxed?" His voice is way softer.

"Why even ask?"

"So I'll write a check." She slowly shakes her head at him. "Is that supposed to mean something?"

"It means," she says, "our so-called checking account is worthless."

"Come on. There's at least, at least—"

"At least zero, Kenny. Less than. We have a house payment due in two days and zilch in our checking account. Just dead air."

"That's ridiculous," he says, "last time I—"

"I've paid bills, sweetheart. There's nothing coming in. It's not too complicated. Subtraction without addition, pretty basic stuff."

"Okay, it's been slow." He swallows.

"Oh," she says, "slow. Well that's okay because the foreclosure will be fast."

"Hey Rain In Da Face," says Bugs Bunny, scrubbing his back with a long-handled brush, "trow anudda log on da fire."

"Fire," says Lorna, "don't touch!"

Kenny looks at the weak achy smile his wife is giving him and his face starts to darken up. "You know, any chance you've ever had to belittle me and my career you've, you've—grabbed at it like a chocolate bon-bon."

"How did I belittle you? I've always supported you no matter how—"

"Yeah, that's right, honey. No matter how stupid and blundering I am. Well, it's like I always say: that's whatcha get for marrying a harelip."

"Oh, Kenny," she says with the saddest shake of the head. "Why do you do that to yourself?"

"Ehhhhhh. What's cookin, Doc?" sniffs Bugs.

"Cookie," says Liza, clapping her little hands.

"I don't know," says Kenny. "Just born dumb I guess." Now he's the one with the far off eyes and, with pity and reproach mixed together in her voice, Allie Smold speaks her husband's name once more. He stands up and announces he's goin out. "I'm not hungry." Kenny pats his little girls on their heads and walks out the house.

"Rabbit stew!" cries Bugs, "That's me!"

"That's me!" says Lorna.

Before he climbs in his SUV Kenny stops and fingers the thick black hairs of his mustache like he's afraid they might of fell out. Well, I can't lie: with the June sun still throwin down rays from high above the rooftops, it's pretty plain to see, through the whiskers: that old pink scar that slants across the independent insurance agent's left lip, while the right half jerks upward now in a twisted little smile of self-cruelty.

If I was a person wanted to retire, take it easy'n live worry-free, what I'd do is I'd get me a place at the Pleasant Prairies Assisted Living up on 18th Street and 4th Avenue, just west of the Good Samaritan Hospital and the Medical Arts Building. Well, I ain't got that option, as you know, but that's what Janet's folks done, and it's swanky. You got your nice little apartment, your fancy dining room with that chef that comes around to see if you like his creations *de jour*, you got book clubs, yoga, every pastime you can think of, even bus trips to Pioneer Village. What else does a person need? You're with old folks, sure. And some ain't in the best of shape, but the majority is pretty sprightly, you'd be surprised. Some of the gals is still—well, nevermind, I'm getting away from the main point. Which is that every Wednesday night Janet comes and joins her folks for dinner, which is complimentary on the house, they can bring a guest along once a week. And tonight's the night.

"Hi, sweetheart," says her mom as Janet kisses her and comes into their snug little assisted living room, which is tidy as a model in a home furniture outlet. "I'm glad you're early. He's been having a bad day. Saw something in the paper that upset him, he won't say what it was. He even shouted at the person on the phone when he called to validate his credit card."

"Hmmh. Mom, what's that smell?"

"What smell, Dear?"

"A weird chemical smell, Mom. Bad, I don't know." The newspaper gal is right. It smells of crusty nickels and pennies inside of an old soup can.

"I don't smell anything, sweetheart. I've been spraying air freshener whenever we—you know. There shouldn't be any bad odors."

"What air freshener? When did you get air freshener?"

"That air freshener with the trees and flowers on it. You know." Mom points to the shelf in the open bathroom.

"Mom! That's surface disinfectant, that's not air freshener, you can't spray that in the air, it's poison. That's just for—you spray that on a surface and wipe it off!"

Mom looks pretty hurt. "Well, I'm sorry dear. It has trees and flowers on it, I thought—. I won't do it anymore." For ten or twelve seconds it's pretty quiet in the apartment except for the TV over in the bedroom. "You better go in and see him, maybe you can settle him down a little. Oh, for dinner they're serving chicken fried steak."

"How funny," Janet says, with her eyes tilting off just a hair right of center.

"Chicken fried steak is funny?"

"No, not really, Mom."

The feller watchin the six o'clock news in the bedroom might be thought, at a glance, to have fell asleep and forgot to close his eyes, except one thing says he ain't: the left forefinger is busy rubbin the cuticles of the left thumb over and over, never stopping, almost like a piston in a old steam engine. And, once or twice we see them crinkled eyes blink. But his daughter comes in, asks "Whatcha thinking about, Dad?" and kisses him, and it's like a old black and white photo somehow comes to life. He is that feller in the photos. Them photos on the wall of Janet's office? Only the crew cut's turned gray and the short-sleeved dress shirt and tie fit a little too loose on the old news man.

It's commercial break on the TV, and there's an ad for that new improved pill for type 2 diabetes. Mr. Hinderson has one of them faces with a brand of wisdom written on it as he smiles and squints up at his daughter. "There's only one thing to think about, sweetheart," and the shortest word was the one he hammered. Janet, before she sits down on the bed, puts hands to hips, blows out a deep gust of air and gives him one of them "Now, now" looks. She tries for a few minutes to buoy up his mood somewhat, but Dad's got a burr in his bonnet about somethin. Turns out he thinks the credit card company is out to get him.

"Dad," she tries to reason, "credit card companies are big impersonal things, why would they have anything against—"

"I'll show you why," he says and, while the TV flashes pictures of the Sky High Bacon Double Burger from Bargain Burger, the old feller scoots his chair just a bit and leans over his tiny glass-top desk and rustles through some papers spread out there. He fishes up a letter and hands it to his daughter. It's one of them letters with gummy stuff where the credit card stuck.

She reads silent for twenty seconds or so and then "Dad, they're not trying to pull a fast one on you. They say that your account number may have been illegally stolen as a result of a merchant database compromise. So they've issued you this new card with a new account number. You just have to call this number and—"

"And that's where the scam comes in, doll." By golly, thanks to a new once-a-day inhaler medicine for COPD, the feller on the tube can take his grandson river rafting like he used to, that's certainly a—anyway Doll, I mean Janet, exhales another lungful before she can muster up the energy to get to the bottom of what's eatin her dad. He's got a theory they made the whole thing up. "How do I know there was a security incident? Tell me that."

"Dad, why would they—"

"It's all about selling insurance, doll. It's about ripping off an old man." While Janet tries to get through to her dad and understand how insurance has came into this credit card situation, the TV's got one of them snazzy cars racing around tight curves while a deep voice says "German engineering" like he's tryin to seduce somebody. "They tried to sell me insurance," Dad repeats, "they tried to sneak it in there because I'm an old man and they think we're all senile."

Out in the living room Mom sets on the plaid sofa and straightens things on the coffee table that was already straight to my eyes, while she listens to the sounds from the bedroom and tries sniffin the air for somethin that ain't trees and flowers afterall.

A short and kinda elderly bundled-up lady tramps into the Foodway Supermarket and stands gaping at the checkout gal for pert'ner five seconds. "Theraflow," is all she finally croaks out, like old codgers lost in the desert call for water in them corny old flicks.

The checkout gal points over her right shoulder while she scans TV dinners with her left hand. "Aisle nine, Mrs. Curtis." The lady wends her way in that direction, each step weaker than the one before. She passes aisle eight which is the baby aisle, and two-thirds down it stands Kenny running his index finger over all the glittering varieties of the latest in disposable diapers. Kenny's cooled down some, I would imagine, after driving up and down the highway a few times, and he ain't cussing out loud but I can see his lips moving kinda indelicate. Just as that supermarket announcer alerts us about firm, succulent avocados from sunny Paraguay which are now two for a dollar on aisle one while supplies last, Kenny throws up his hands and yanks a jumbo pack of Scampers from the shelf and heads to the front. He stops short when he gets to the line cause the two fellas at the end of it are

Cosetti and Laertes Norris. They each got a six-pack and are tryin not to let on that they recognize the guy with the diapers. Kenny don't let em off so easy and starts up a conversation, but they manage to get their beer paid for and make their getaway before the word "underwrite" ever has a chance to pop up. This second brush-off don't do much to enhance Kenny's mood, so when the checker asks him if he found everything okay Kenny ain't the pleasantest guy in the world.

"Not really, Maria. I wanted the Googies with the Supersleek Lightweight Material, the Safe and Comfy Fit Design, Cozy-stretch Waistband, Designer Graphics, Extra-absorbant No-leak Pads, Triple-grip Reseal Strips, and the Color-code Wetness Gauge. But you don't have em." What can a checker do with a regular customer like that except stand and blink and pull her jaw back up?

"Vern!" she yells out the corner of her mouth in the direction of the assistant manager's counter next to the charcoal briquettes. Right behind Kenny shivers the bundled-up lady with her Theraflow, coughing up a fit all over his ninety-five dollar dress shirt.

By the time Kenny comes out into the muggy parking lot, darkness has fell and he squints against them bright pinky white lights overhead. His keys are out and his thumb is ready to beep-beep his car open when he looks to his left and the limo's there at the far end of the lot and somethin ain't right over there. There's voices, coupla strangers movin about, and by gad there's a robbery goin on! Things is kinda turvy and goin down fast so it ain't too easy to make out what's what exactly but. The driver's door is ajar with the window down and Laertes and Steve is both in the front seat with their hands up and lookin remarkably calm like they'd practiced this for weeks, and tryin I think to pacify them two robbers somewhat. You'd think these two particular strangers was a pair of expectant hens, as nervous as they act, speakin Spanish and English so fast and so mixed that what comes out is jambalaya. The rascal with the gun wears a bright Harvard T-shirt and his trigger hand quivers like an arrow in the breeze. His partner has got the two six-packs under his arms, and is lookin around every five seconds to make sure they ain't surrounded. His shirt says Alabama Crimson Tide, and has old blood stains front and back. Both fellas got red gunk wedged deep under their fingernails.

Kenny don't yell or nothin but I guess his fast-approaching footsteps with them diapers under his arm distract the two rascals, and whilst they turn to look Laertes makes a move for his gun stashed quite handy under the dashboard. Now: I wisht I could somehow or some way tell you what exactly happens next, but I can't. It is too quick and too hectic for an old sodface like me to figure out with any degree of accurateness. All's I can tell you for sure is that there's a whole lot of fumbling of weapons and somehow—again, I haven't the foggiest—Harvard ends up with Laertes' gun and Laertes ends up with Harvard's. Then, what comes next is a blur, but there's at least two, maybe three, flashes and explosions and yelps of pain, grunts, shouts, and things that sound like splat. Then—and this is the only part that ain't in doubt whatsoever—them diapers, the whole jumbo pack, is suddenly flyin through the warm night air toward Bama's icy face with all the fury that a riled-up independent insurance agent can summon.

When Janet gets home from dinner with her folks she grabs the mail and sets down on her couch under the yellow lamp while Scoop flops at her feet and plants his grizzled chin and paws upon them. The junk mail pile is big and the proper mail pile is small when Janet comes upon a letter that looks awful familiar. She sets up straight and stares at the envelope, and in a low breathy voice she says some words that don't sound so nice, but they ain't really meant for anyone's ears, so I'll disregard. Anyways, she tears open that envelope and, well I told you she's a fast reader. About forty-five seconds later she's callin the activation number on the card, and it don't take long before Janet's out-and-out screamin at the customer service rep and threatenin to lodge a complaint with the FTC in Washington. And I got a pretty good hunch that tomorrow morning Peg Rossiter'll have a brand new assignment: some kind of story on credit card companies. And how they've been pullin a bunch of fast ones on people in the cities, across the prairies, and everywhere else there is.

Well, if we learned one thing tonight, it's that a jumbo pack of Scampers diapers can stop a .38 caliber bullet at twenty feet. And, if hurled with enough ginger by a feller who was in a sour mood to begin with even before gettin shot at, it can knock out a bad guy who's high on medium-grade methamphetamine. Plus seven beers. Make that two things.

By the time Laertes gets to the Good Samaritan Hospital E.R., his boss is stitched up and resting pretty comfortable, with thick pressure bandages on the side where the bullet went through and a little half-pint of orange juice in his hand. "Guess what," says Laertes, with a lowered voice and furtive glance at Kenny in the gurney cross the aisle, who's staring over their way with a blissful kind of expression which mayn't be entirely due to the painkillers he was give. There's a young nurse wrapping up Kenny's shoulder, the one that he heaved them diapers with.

"The bastards got away." But Cosetti's grin ain't destined for longevity as it crumbles pretty quick into a fit of hurtful coughing. "Aghhh," groans the poor feller as the nurse trots over to check his dressing.

The ex-Husker looks down with pity on his boss while the nurse fiddles around and probes whatever it is she thinks ain't been prodded or probed enough times already. Meanwhile, Kenny continues to stare kinda enraptured from his stretcher, so Laertes gives him a hefty smile. "How's your shoulder, man?"

"They popped it back in." Kenny ain't blinked in quite some time.

"You're a crazy dude, you know that?" says Laertes. Kenny just shakes his head once or twice real slow and then essentially replies Nah: he just don't like the idea of innocent people being ripped off of what they've worked hard for. Kenny don't usually sound like John Wayne, but I guess it could be the morphine. "Well," says Laertes, "it was lucky for us you showed up, dude. You made it three on two, you know. Three on two is always an advantage, man."

Anyways, when the nurse trots back over Kenny's way Laertes leans down and, speakin pretty confidential, assures Cosetti that Sheriff Wendy's got the outlaws shackled like a chain gang, and they're spilling their guts as we speak. "But," and he flings another guarded glance toward Kenny's vicinity, "you're not gonna like it, boss." Cosetti don't have to say What, he's got one of them faces. "Those two scalawags work for us, boss."

That there piece of intelligence don't seem to register for a few seconds with Cosetti, then finally his one eye narrows and he mutters a word suitable for the moment. But not for broadcast. "Where?" he says after a bit, in a voice that's chiseled flintrock.

"Riverside plant, mostly graveyard." Well, this time Cosetti picks the other suitable word that was left over from last time. Laertes pulls a scrap of paper from his wallet and reads off the names, in as near a whisper as the big guy can git: Marco Antonio Zamora, he reads, that was Harvard the triggerman. Victor Hugo Castaneda was Bama, the lookout fella. Job descriptions according to their company I.D.'s that was found on em: Harvard, he's a Grade II Slaughterer, job is to perform needle lobotomy or sever jugular. Bama is a Grade I Slaughterer, job's to skin the animal, sever head and body parts, eviscerate and trim the carcass. Both is been at the plant upwards of five years, according to what Laertes found out.

"You know what kind of field day she's gonna have with this?" says Cosetti, his voice low and gritty. "Mmmh. We're sunk, hot shot. I can see the headline now."

"No way she's gonna find out, boss. Not til it's too late. I had me a little talk with Wendy—uh, Sheriff Healy. She says she'll keep the entire incident under wraps til Monday evening, after the council meeting. In the interest of ongoing investigation, she says. We're frickin heroes. These two bozos are meth heads, boss, they're gonna lead her to the exact location of the drug lab that she wants to bust more than anything. And I don't mind telling you," big guys sometimes look goofy when they get dreamy-eyed, "she gave me a kiss I won't forget for—well, I don't know how long, to be honest with you."

"Okay, Mr. Cosetti," says Dr. Chowdhury, not quite shouting and appearing out of nowhere, "we will have you out of here straightaway. Nurse will be in to go over the discharge papers directly." Doc's got kind of a brisk and lilty way with his words, you know. Which I spose is the way most folks talk back east in Doc's hometown of Calcutta. "You just do the needful, are we clear? Take it easy for next twenty-four hours. No lifting," and he does a spreading thing with his hands like a umpire calling safe. Doc had to wait to finish speaking before he can smile. But a handsome smile.

So Steve hints around to Dr. Chowdhury, in so many words, that he sure don't want this shooting incident leaking out to the public. "Not to worry, Mr. Cosetti. I'm sworn." Steve kind of apologizes then, says he was stupid to mention it, any first-year law student knows the physician-patient privilege. "You're a lawyer, Mr. Cosetti?"

"You've heard of the Fifth Amendment, Doc?"

"Ah, that's a good one, Mr. Cosetti." Doc gets a kick out of that one, to the point that his voice starts to squeak. "You better believe I know the Fifth Amendment, I watch reruns of Dragnet on my days off. I have seen every episode thoroughly twiceover."

Doc vanishes and Cosetti's demeanor seems to have brightened up a bit, until he looks over and sees Kenny settin there propped up in wide-eyed euphoria. You know, a feller don't necessarily appreciate it when the smirk that ought to be on his own face shows up on somebody else's.

Exhaustion got the better of Lark at some point in them wee hours—she's only human ain't she. So sleep she did. But every little while the Sioux maiden awakes in this snug Arapaho teepee and her eyes got to dart around a bit to recollect where she is and the mishaps that got her there. Then they turn kinda disappointed beneath a furrowed brow but little by little the brow smoothes out nice and them eyes take on a almost peaceful aspect as they stare at the two old Arapaho aunties betwixt which her bedroll's laid. Only a trace of soft moonlight seeps through the stretched buffalo skins of the teepee, and sleep soon folds her brave eyelids like tender blankets over tuckered-out tots.

Thursday

*N*eon signs are sorta hard to read in daylight when they're turned off. Jever notice that? So motel owner Lyle Griff decided by golly he'd turn on his Best Midwestern sign this morning. Well, in fact it's almost dark enough. And out of that dark sky in the last two or three minutes has come big fat raindrops, which sizzle when they hit the halogen floodlights in the shrubbery all around the sign. Now Lyle is mainly absorbed in nudging Cosetti, gradually you see, over to just the right spot in front of the Kids Stay Free sign, which flashes every three and a half seconds. A press conference needs a proper backdrop, don't you know.

Cosetti, I guess, is used to folks prodding and nudging him around, with his one eye situation and all, but how can he bury every single trace of pain when Lyle nudges too close to that place that got shot? His two interns are by his side, plus a bearded fella looks vaguely familiar, dressed almost as swanky as Cosetti. Everybody's hunkered under their umbrellas, of various shapes and sizes. The press corps is there in force: Janet, Rossiter, and the *Cat* photographer under big black umbrellas, and the KOTT sound gal and news guy beneath a portable awning contraption. The entire motel housekeeping staff is behind them, uncovered, but as the wind and rain picks up them folks start to flee. Off to the side is Sheriff Healy and Laertes, under one small umbrella and not too awful interested in anything outside of that umbrella. Probly discussing the '06 K-State Nebraska game, which was a humdinger. Sure. Traffic-wise it's pretty sparse out here on the outskirts of West Cottonwood Way, but now and again a car with lights and wipers on high will slow down to see what's what.

Everybody looks slightly peeved at standing in the rain, and Rossiter keeps pestering her boss about why don't they move this garden party inside.

Her boss, on the other hand, don't seem quite here, editorially speaking. You'd think Janet's covering the funeral of the guy who invented quotation marks by the way her face looks: like two semicolons squished together. And her body: a wilted question mark. Like she's aiming to burrow under that there umbrella if she can and never come out. Ain't like her.

"Okay, we'll make this quick," announces Cosetti and, cept for Janet, the press snaps to attention. Cosetti coughs once or twice and winces with pain but tries keepin it under his belt so to speak while he introduces the bearded gent. Now, you may never have thought that there's such a calling in this world as North American Tree Carving Analyst—and Rossiter's face shows pretty clear that she's never heard of any such thing when Cosetti says it—but apparently here he stands and his name is Mr. Colin Krolak, PhD, and he's the leading expert in the country and. Well. Say. Now that I get a better look at the fella as he tilts his umbrella up and assumes a grave demeanor, there ain't no doubt. Twenty years can alter a person but if you was here and you had Janet's copy of her old year-end edition from college, you would almost certain agree this is that same serious fella. The one beside her in the picture. Not that Janet is looking, cause she ain't. She's hid in that umbrella and kinda paralyzed I think. But shivering.

Well, the tree carving doc starts explaining his findings the way a judge pronounces sentence, and it seems the arborglyph found up on O.G.'s neighbor is a cheap hoax. The carving was made to look aged, says Krolak, the prankster used pure maple syrup for the effect. He could smell the maple syrup ten feet away. Underneath the syrup the carving was fresh as new lumber from a sawmill. Cosetti now, he's glancing towards Janet's umbrella and grinning but it's kind of a disappointed grin since he can't see nothing whatsoever of the publisher's reaction.

Well, what with the rain and wind fiercer by the second, Rossiter and the KOTT news guy each ask one question, then Krolak steps back solemnly and Sheriff Healy steps up and announces that Felony Vandalism charges will be brought against the young suspect as soon as—. Steve quickly whispers in the sheriff's ear, and Sheriff Healy throws a questioning glance at Laertes. Laertes nods and she smiles a sweet unsheriffy smile. "Misdemeanor Vandalism charges will be brought against the young—" Steve leans in again and whispers. Sheriff gets another reassuring nod, and swallows. "No charges will be brought against the suspect. The young perpetrator will be referred for counseling." Well—Justice, they say, is blind. But She hears pretty good.

Anyways, they wrap up the press conference pronto. Folks is ready to dash for shelter when a big lashing gust of wind wallops the area. The squall batters everybody and Janet's umbrella almost flies from her hands and pops clean inside-out. There she stands under the stinging rain in a state of shock tryin to resurrect her poor parasol, and the fella Krolak does a double take.

"Janet?" he says, staring at her drippiness, demanding to know is it really her, and if it is what she's doing here at his press conference. "It hadn't occurred to me," says the fella while he strokes his beard in meditative fashion, "that you live here." Well, Janet tries puttin a brave face to that and says what she can that might halfway establish that she's not a stalker or a homeless bum, then he nods and favors her with a weighty saga: how he was boarding his flight from Tallahassee to Portland where he has his consulting firm and lives with his wife and four children ages eighteen to ten when they paged him to do a stopover in Nebraska, since he's the only recognized expert in the lower forty-eight. And while he further edifies Janet with his impressive resume, she stands under her collapsed umbrella with a look that says Please God I just wanna shrivel up and wash down the nearest storm drain. Finally Rossiter crowds in, umbrellas her boss, taps her foot on the wet asphalt and glowers. Lyle Griff, promising coffee and sweet rolls, leads Sheriff Healy and the Euphemion folks toward the motel lobby. Steve Cosetti almost trips on a ornamental rock, lets out a cry of pain and grabs his side. Poor fella. He needs to watch where he's going, I would say, not be lookin backwards at people standing in the rain.

With newsprint on their fingertips and the morning's *Caterwauler* in shambles, Milt, Ray, and Bill has just about given up. Given up on Nickano Jr. ever whistling that new country tune in a better key than the one he orchestrates while he bangs things around in that kitchen of his. And, given up on their missing fourth wheel when in he rolls.

Ray stifles a yawn and picks up the Farm News section to make room, and Kenny slides in and don't say a word while they stare. Number one: Kenny's already been to the barber and spruced up, which ain't all that abnormal for Kenny. But number two, with his right arm hangin down, his shoulder's all poofy under the shirt and, while Ray pours, he holds his coffee mug in his manicured left hand. Then three, there ain't hardly a trace this morning of sarcasm nor scorn in Kenny's smile: the independent agent looks for the first time in a long time like he might actually be what you could brand as happy.

Why would a guy be so chipper just because he strained his shoulder lifting weights? is what Milt seems to be thinking when Kenny gives him that scenario as a excuse. Milt eyes Kenny's bony frame suspiciously and finally he lights up all lurid like a red fox on the prowl. "Somebody got lucky last night and got a little too frisky, didn't they?"

Kenny gives a sheepish shrug of his one good shoulder and opens that hand like it's got Milt's bank deposit in it. "You got me, Milt. You know me too well, you old dog."

"Yeah I knew it, you sly rascal. Sock it to me, eh!" Milt tops off Kenny's coffee with glee. Well, they're a jubilant bunch for the rest of their coffee break though nobody says another word about Kenny's shoulder. Kenny announces everything's on him today, and he even calls back to Nickano Jr. that he wants a dozen assorted scones and muffins to take home. Nickano Jr. found a new key to whistle at, one of them keys that mostly you only hear from your local high school orchestra.

Well, an hour or so after the press conference finds the precip startin to let up and the City of Cottonwood wearin a green glittery gown to welcome the sun back, as Steve sets in his limo outside of the Stucko Fasteners manufacturing plant out east of town near the fairgrounds and checks off the name Laura Ryder who happens to own that company and is name number two on that little memo on his phone. Then he speed dials, while he adjusts the pillow under his side, and gets Janet on the horn to see when she's planning on printing a retraction.

"There's nothing to retract. We—"

"Right, you only said it's under investigation. I get that. So now that we know the outcome of that investigation—"

"Of course we're printing the outcome, Mr. Cosetti. But that's not all we're reporting." For a couple seconds it's like she has to let herself just breathe. "There's a human interest side to this thing, too. I don't expect your company to understand."

Cosetti don't say anything but just sets in his limo with a uneasy look. Cause there's a flatness in Janet's voice, that ain't never been there before. And after the two of them hang up she just sets kinda sunken at her desk. In a brown study, as they used to say in them old classic stories. She stares at her computer screen but there ain't one ounce of feeling—what you'd call life—in her right now. No more than that empty wastebasket at her feet. At least not so far as you can see from the outside. I hate to think what might be wastin away on Janet's inside.

Young gals with babies in cradle boards on their backs, older gals burdened with camp gear, all slow their pace and come to a gradual halt. Kids playin the Arapaho hoop game over the plains catch their spinning hoops and stop to stare. Fellers with eyes peeled for buffalo tracks or for danger tense their muscles and exchange signals and ready words. Headin eastward with the Platte River always in sight, Chief White Raven's village ain't met up with any buffalo yet this morning, but they've got company. Fast approachin is a small band of strangers, and these fellas and the Arapaho ain't always on the best of terms.

Lark Laying Eggs, who's spent the morning meandering these grassy lowlands with the Arapaho and hauling her share of the load, shields her eyes from the sun and is as curious as anyone. As the strangers grow near so that their looks and manner of dress is quite evident, Lark begins to smile a careful smile—and it's the only smile in the neighborhood right now. While the other gals hang back, she edges up closer and soon the words that these unfamiliars speak amongst theirselves can just be made out. They come up face to face with Chief White Raven and all the leaders of his village, and pretty soon there's a full-fledged pow-wow.

Well, through sign language and knowin some of one another's lingo, the two parties engage in various parleys and summits, and Lark is standin there the whole time particularly engrossed in the proceedings. Then it starts to become kinda apparent that she's the thing that they're mainly all discoursing about, and she pretty quick gets self-conscious of herself and even quicker hides that little smile away. Yup, them strangers is eyeing her like she's breakfast on the stove, and Chief White Raven comes and fetches her and brings her to the middle of that conference.

Now, that looks scary, don't it? And Lark looks duly petrified and timid—in the midst of this lively debate—as she should. But thanks to her sis, Lark knows pretty good Pawnee, which is what these new fellers is. And she may be able to fool these folks, but I can tell you for a fact that beneath that anxious crease of her features, she's one happy lady. Finally, the chief looks up and there's an eagle spiraling way above, and to the Arapaho that's the most sacred of all creatures, messenger to the Great Spirit. The best omen there is.

"Done!" says the chief, and maybe Lark ought to be insulted that she been traded to these Pawnee scouts for a couple raccoon pelts and a old dog, but her woeful act don't altogether camouflage a teensy-weensy grin that wants to pluck at the corners of her mouth.

Well, the Pawnee scouts take Lark, do an about-face, and head east at a crisp pace. The Arapahoe decide to turn south, toward friendlier hunting grounds. And that eagle swoops low, scatters a rabbit or two, and flies off to dizzy heights over the big flat muddy river.

She's in a awful rush. Known fact. You're gonna have to trust me on this. If you want physical evidence, there ain't any. You can't tell by lookin at her, cause her features is no less lifeless than grandmamma's portrait in some crusty old mansion. And she'd have to smear glue on the soles of her orthopedic sandals to go any slower down these wide cleanswept sidewalks of Platte Avenue. Mosey would be a step up. But Florene is always anxious to get back from lunch whenever Warren R. Kessler's left in charge. Good shoe salesman, Warren, but not quite executive material.

So be it, rush or no rush, nothin don't alter Florene's personality. "Hey, Carol," says she, pokerfaced, "how's that new granddaughter of yours?" Granddaughter's doin fine, and Carol's got the proof right there on her phone as she stops and hangs her purse and her shopping bags on the fifty cent horsey ride in front of Bide-a-Wee Children's Wear. That smile might be Florene's first facial expression of the day.

"I like your tie, Walt," says Flo as she passes DeVille Pharmacy, "goes better than that beige one. Say hello to Barbara for me."

"Hi, Eddie!" Florene's hands, a little like shoe leather themselves, have gone to her hips and she gazes upwards at a massive blond head and wary, roving blue eyes. "How're you getting along? How's your aunt?"

"She's good, Mrs. Wallace, yeah." Deputy Banacek licks the entire inside of his big lower lip like he's hankerin for a shot of whisky at high noon, and scans the broad avenue for gunslingers of any hue. "Mom says Aunt Erica's pelvis is coming along pretty well and she should be up and around soon. Praise the Lord."

"Is she coming up for reunion next year?"

"That I don't know, Mrs. Wallace, I—do you have a minute?" His tongue takes another pasty tour inside that lip as he scours every direction for spies, including up. Florene being somewhat less than regulation size, Deputy Banacek loosens his holster belt in order that he can lean from the waist and whisper. Well, Florene don't register any emotion whatsoever as she's escorted around the corner toward his patrol car. But Evelyn Westcott seems mighty surprised when she waves at Flo from across the street and don't get so much as a howdie-do.

He ain't had major supporting roles in two class plays and a school musical for nothing, and the *Cat* photographer seems pretty tickled with his half-dozen dramatic headshots of Keith on his living room couch. But the real drama is Mrs. O'Conner at the other end of the couch, whose white fingers cradle her inflamed cheeks and whose eyes plead with the disbelief and the tragedy of a son who just graduated high school and already is halfway down the path to infamy, prison and, almost for sure, the electric chair.

"Ms. Rossiter, we feel that trees—"

"Who's 'we'?"

"I—I meant I," says Keith. "We in the abstract."

"You had friends helping you?" Peg catches the photographer's eye, and there is contact. I spose when conspiracy is lurking about, it takes one to know one.

"No, I—did this all on my own." He says it with a Lindbergh kind of smile. His poor mom is shakin her head, not believing what she's seeing and hearing from her mild-mannered son.

Rossiter nods for a bit, then fixes wide hypnotic eyes on Keith. "You felt desperate. You felt powerless to stop something you believed morally wrong."

"That's exactly wha—"

"You were so desperate you were willing to maim a beloved cottonwood in order to save them all from destruction. You were driven to risk your reputation, your future, to protect the abiding values that make our community a special place in America." For a split second only, she glances down at her recorder on the coffee table next to the gilded picture frame with Keith and his two older sisters dressed up swanky. Keith doesn't speak, his pale lips hang apart and he nods his wavy head and points a ratifying finger at whatever's in that little reporter's notebook in Peg's hand.

By the time the young man comforts and subdues the pitiful sobbing at the other end of the couch, Rossiter and her photographer are packed up and pert'ner out the door.

With upraised eyes declaring himself neither friendly, unfriendly, nor a speck bothered by the distinction, one of these fellers makes signs for her to fill up her water flask in the cold river like he was doing hisself. Another young feller give her a nice fat corn cake, somethin she ain't had that much opportunity to partake back home. Lark smiles and looks back over the frothy river she and her fleetfooted escorts'd just forded. Them Arapahos of Chief White Raven is clean out of sight. She blows out a pretty long flurry of air and lets her shoulders unhitch. "Thanking you," she says in the best Pawnee she can assemble. "I am happy to be find of you."

Well, nothin happens for a second or two after she speaks, but then them Pawnee scouts do a sharp double-take and some of their tonsils get a rare look at the sun. One big feller walks right up into Lark's face. "Don't tell me you're one of us, Princess, a regular Human Being?" says the fierce warrior, running his hands up the smooth shaved sides of his skull. "That's not how we heard it. The Arapaho swore you're a big chief's daughter. Am I right, boys? They carried you off in a gutsy coup up on the Snake River. Two moons ago, snow on the ground. Said they utterly decimated the toughest and meanest Sioux camp east of the Black Hills. Said their grandchildren will be telling the story to their grandchildren." He sweeps his proud forehead left and then right and his dozen or so confederates, their sinewy arms encasing hearty chests, exchange severe nods in affirmation of that there gospel.

"My sister Pawnee she!"

Um, that little outburst echoes off the low bluffs, the big dude tilts his head and tries to shake his ears out, and a great gray flock of sandhill cranes launches skyward from across the river. There's one a them hundred dollar words, ain't there, if I could just untangle the right cobweb, for a gal that's got volumes to tell and the guy she's tellin keeps lookin at his watch. How do you make em listen?

"I some walk to here some days many. Reason for so if help my Pawnee sister." The big feller, goes by the name of Hill Seeker, shifts his weight once or twice and gives a quizzical look around at his shrugging cohorts. Well somehow or other, somehow, with the preface that there wasn't no fight and nobody captured nobody, Lark manages to get her story across in fair halting Pawnee. While these Pawnee pathfinders inch up closer, lookin self-conscious and a little like they shoulda peed before they left home, she churns out her whole half-baked plan: which was to find Running Water's kin and get them to swap herself to the Oglala and return Running Water back to her people before she has to marry old Chief Rain Bear. Hmmmh.

For the last two to three minutes the big rascal has stood stock still, squinting one eye upwards at white drifting streaks, the other eye closed tight, and his open jaw jutting in and out of joint like he's got the theory of metaphysics almost figured out.

"Say, you talk pretty good Pawnee for a foreigner," says one of the other young fellers, stepping forward and adjusting the array of scalps fastened to his leggings to their best advantage. "Where did you—"

"Please. Me must of now must of bring to family sister Pawnee. Running Water. Family where? Must of bring. Help to sister. Bad marriage."

"Listen, Little Sister," says another Pawnee scout who's got him a deep husky voice and looks straight up at Lark from a panther-like crouch. He points to the owl feathers sproutin from the narrow scalplock atop his shaved head. "Do you see snow on this head?" She looks where he points but don't seem to savvy. "How many winters line my face? Hmhhh? You're not getting me." He turns to his fellows. "She's not getting me. Look, Little Sister: it takes more winters than you can count to become a chief of the greatest people on the plains. All of us here, we're just working our way up. Our job is to deliver you to our village, period. The chiefs will take it from there."

"That's the point," says big Hill Seeker, who's snapped out of whatever stupor he was in, "the chiefs will take it from there."

"Whatever beef you got," says Crouching Panther Who Speaks With Deep Voice, which strangely enough happens to be the fella's name, "you take it up with them."

"Don't worry, my little Evening Star. You will be nicely looked after." This lean young feller has come forward who ain't been heard from yet, but all his brothers suddenly get quiet and take a step sideways to open a path for the dude. "You don't need to stand there like a yearling buffalo cornered by wolves." This feller talks pretty good despite a well-chewed oakwood pipe stuck in his mouth and a nervous twitch of both eyes and the nose along with em. A edgy kind of sidewinder, he imparts a strange fidgety smile around to his onlooking troops, while Lark I guess tries to figger out the dude's metaphors in her head. She watches him take his pipe out, look kinda long and ironic at the cold tobacco in its carved stone bowl, and then cast the same look among his men. The chipper young fella who gave pretty fair marks to Lark in Introductory Pawnee, well they call him Little Brother and Little Brother jumps to attention, pulls two chunks of pyrite from his pouch, and within seconds has sparked enough tinder to give a good glow to that pipe notwithstanding the twitchy hand that grasps it.

Now, while he puffs his pipeful and seems to simmer down some, I don't know if this antsy dude purposely brandishes his long war lance in Lark's face or if he's just slightly forgetful, but he's got her attention, that's one thing. "Ah," he says, "I see you're curious about my trophies, Evening Star." Yup, from the throat of the man's spearhead dangle a pair of scalps, swaying in the river-scented breeze. The same breeze, matter of fact, that sifts through the blackness of Lark's shouldered hair.

"My name no Evening Star. Name from me was—"

"Oh. No, no, you misconstrue. I was only greeting the evening star, Little Sister. See," says he pointing and just barely twitching, "she sits in the west as we speak." While Lark turns a hasty glance toward the dipping sun where Venus is in fact closely hovering, this lean Pawnee lieutenant known as Left Hand winks at his men. And there was a pretty droll joke in there somewhere, if their reaction's any gauge. "Since you're so curious, I won't keep you in anticipation any longer, Little Sister. This," he says jabbing an index finger at a dangling scalp with long stringy gray hair, "was an old woman of the Cheyenne. She was hiding her grandson in her bosom. This," and he shifts his finger to the tiny curly scalp sharing his lancehead, "was the grandson."

If you think any of that was lost in translation, then you ain't seen Lark's eyes. Or heard the clutch in her throat as she states, after a prayer-like silence, that the Cheyenne are her people's friends.

Left Hand smiles as he shoulders his lance, checks his gear, and rises to his full height. His comrades take the cue and no more'n ten seconds later the whole patrol is ready to make tracks. "You are our honored guest, Little Sister. That's all you really need to know."

Them big graceful cranes float back down to their northbound restin place and Lark and her bodyguards kick out hup-two on their eastward march like it's crosscountry season at the varsity state finals and the crack of the starter pistol just broke an unbearable tension.

"No, Ida," says Florene, gliding a low-heeled pump onto Ida Sweetzer's right 7½ narrow, "that was Gil Mason, Dan's older brother. Gil's the one who married Owen Stanley's second oldest daughter who sold carpeting at Wacklund's for a while. Dan's married to that Carla Lanterman from North Platte. She—well anyway, Dan was gettin a detail job on his Camero over at Stickler's Detail, and Merv Stickler was selling new seat covers to Susie Lapides, and Dan overheard Susie tell Merv that—oh, hey Janet."

The funny thing is, Janet come right through that front door of Florene's store without so much as a tinkle from that little bell. It don't seem possible, even Flo herself on a slow day can't come and go without a jingle of some sort. But then, this ain't the Janet I know. This Janet has got me worried to the gills. With her pasty cheeks and lost eyes. Florene signals to Janet to sit herself down and wait til she's free, and I'll be darned if the news gal doesn't do just that, without a peep of protest. Almost—not quite but almost—like a marionette let go of by some little kid that's cranky and ready for her nap. That's the sorry picture this Janet calls to mind, settin there astraddle one of Florene's fitting stools and waitin for somebody, or some thing, to snap some life into her. Pulling strings may not be enough.

The sun is sank low in the peaked sky. Fingers of it poke through young leaves and old branches to the floor. Not every Pawnee shaves the sides of his head so fierce, cause this stocky fella with shoulders like a stevadore has his hair growed out long, and loose. Which is good right about now since that fresh doeskin poultice plastered across his puffed and purpled cheekbone ain't such a wonderful thing to behold. This here's a small clearing. Sheltered between two tall beauties, a cottonwood on the south and an elm on the north. Imagine what these two trees have seen and shared over the years. Somewhere close by a dove sits still and thoughtful, and rehearses its ageless cradlesong that lullabies me surer than any sound, animal, human or otherwise.

Somebody's gone and shot two arrows into the ground: one at the foot of each of them tall trees. This fella gazes down meditatively. All at once he seizes his hatchet and looks to be aiming a hefty, violent blow at the cottonwood, muttering low and blasphemous. The hatchet freezes midswing, the fella lets out a grunt of anguish. For there's sounds. Footsteps and human forms movin down nearer the river. Can't see much through the growth but one of them shadows moves a little too willowy and wispy and not nothin like a Pawnee brave oughta move. Maybe there's too much sun in the eyes or his swollen cheek has started in throbbing. Or maybe the man don't much care for the little glimpses that smite him through the leaves and branches, in this lush green thread of river stitched across the broad unfurled prairie. I can't really say but. Fella strikes me, as he stumbles back and scowls darkly at the two arrow tips, as somebody who takes things a bit too serious. He throws his thick hands in the air and turns to go.

One of his moccasins don't, it catches and gets left behind on a wild current vine and the fella hops around on one foot for a few seconds until he can yank that moccasin free. No sooner does he get hisself re-shod than he heads out of the clearing. Well, everything's probly—hey young feller look out for that—

Badger hole.

It's nice when you feel comfortable enough with someone that you can tell them things. Personal things. Like don't panic but you've got a big gristly wad of pork stuck in your braces, for instance. And if you can tell em all that without words, just sending meaningful eye signals from across the table and arching your upper lip in the right place so's she'll catch on pretty quick of what the situation is and which tooth her tongue oughta check out before she smiles or anything, well that just shows what good friends you've become and how dang well you know each other. It's nice, that's all.

Well, it's also kinda fortunate that, except for saying how much they like interning for Mr. Cosetti and how much they've learned, interns don't have to speak much when they're out to dinner with their boss and The Greater Cottonwood Chamber of Commerce executive director and the chairman of the board and his wife. The young ladies can pretty much just sit awestruck and watch the conversation like it's reality television, only it's commercial-free. Or is it?

"Excuse me, I'll be right—" says the young lady with dark hair and braces, barely opening her mouth and a little flushed around the eyes. Her fair-haired roommate watches her go toward the ladies' room, and I guess flushes are kinda like yawns. Come to think of it, there really ain't no ladylike way to dislodge a thick chewy strand of ribmeat from your braces while you're settin at the table.

Best table in the house, by the way, at the big southern window. Each table made from the planks of actual cattle ramps dismantled from the old Sioux City stockyards. Sure it's a little pricey, but The Rib Retreat is worth every shekel. Well, those're Milt's words, every time he brings Estelle for lunch. The words that Cosetti uses are "I can't say enough about these spareribs." He's said it about three times. He ain't got nothin stuck in his teeth.

"I wish you could see the nighttime view," says Kelly Waligorski, the chamber's executive director, and then she glances at Cosetti's eyepatch and her face turns kinda appalled, like someone just kicked her under the table. Which, though he may be a pushy guy I don't think Reeves Palmer the board chairman would kick somebody under the table for bad word choice. "It's early yet. Heh, heh." That's not Kelly's real laugh.

Well, Reeves finds a corner of his napkin that don't have barbeque sauce and wipes off his fingertips and his mustache. "Steve," he says, "from up here at the top of this hill you get a view of the whole brilliant span of Cottonwood. And growing every year. If you were to drive into town from up north some evening and come over that hill, you'd see a sight—. Well, no disrespect to Omaha, it's a fine city but I don't think even a big city like Omaha can match our dazzling view. Like a big twinkling Christmas tree: Cottonwood by night."

"I'll tell you what, Reeves," and Cosetti flourishes his half-mowed sparerib in the air like Exhibit A before a jury, "and Kelly. I will make a point of being in Cottonwood at least once a month, and I would love to have dinner with you and the Chamber at this very table and enjoy this beautiful ambiance with you good people."

"You'd have to be a platinum member for that, Steve," and Reeves Palmer winks over at his pretty executive director. "What do you think, Kelly? Is there room in the chamber for Steve here?"

"Oh, I think I could probably pull some strings and get him in." I'm thinkin there must be dimples on both sides of Kelly's family.

"So where do I sign?" says Cosetti's grin.

"What sign? You're in! Right, Kelly?"

"Done deal, Reeves."

Steve keeps from chuckling too hard and busting one of them stitches in his side but he is pretty tickled by all this, and by the time his intern gets back from the ladies' room and starts in on her scalloped potatoes which has had plenty of time to congeal, he's chatting with Mrs. Palmer about what keeps her busy while her husband takes care of his real estate business and chamber activities. Well, besides grandkids of course, turns out she wears two hats, with a florist shop and also a seat on the city council. "So," says Ann Palmer, "between the two, you know—"

"Two hats, huh?" says Steve. I don't know how the conversation gets around to politics eventually, but Steve's a well-spoken guy and he seems to know a lot about lots of different subjects. Chooses his words so well. Makes sure that all this Chamber of Commerce and corporate expansion talk don't exclude Mrs. Palmer so that she would feel left out in the least. Which is thoughtful. There's only a minute or so where Ann Palmer starts to fidget and flush and take big drinks of iced tea. Just around the time when Cosetti goes into a little too much detail about the coincidence of his other hat. Maybe she shoulda done like the interns done: keep a pink sparkly cell phone on the edge of her chair by her thigh and thumb for stray messages with a shy downward gaze.

Well Cosetti don't mind fiddling with his cell phone right out in the open. He can converse perfectly smooth, drink his coffee, and check off name number three all at the same dang time.

She heard tell plenty of times about the Pawnee earth lodges but, a course, seeing how Pawnee and Sioux is mortal foes she ain't never seen one. Til now. And not just one. Pert'ner three dozen in a settlement as lasting and citified as anything on the plains. Each lodge a marvel of wood, grass and, a course, yours truly, fashioned into a spherical redoubt roomy enough for thirty, forty souls to call home.

Dusk and dinnertime and Lark Laying Eggs with her fleetfoot escorts all arrive and pert'ner in unison, to boot. The village is tickled to see all them scouts come back on two feet and with their hairline properly welded. Kids, women, some of the braves come up to ogle. They look more curious than cordial but, forgettin the shaved heads of most of the fellas, not no different, really, than people back in Lark's village. Anyways, once she's over the shock of them earth lodges looming all about and more faces than she's seen in one spot not countin the all-Sioux Sun Dances she been to once't or twice, Lark don't waste no time making her pitch to the chiefly-looking gent who is foremost in the delegation.

But Eagle Chief, with hair like the ashes of a council fire in braids upon his chest, has a sad face made even sadder by Lark's mangled Pawnee. So that hombre what calls hisself Left Hand slides in real close blowing pipe smoke and offering the friendly advice to relax, little Evening Star. "Little Sister, that is." Lefty casts a pasted smile around the throng of his people and sees this odd fella who is hobbling along preoccupied with chewing a stalk of rhubarb and lookin at his moccasins like he just tried em on and he's thinking of taking em on approval. Left Hand grabs the hefty muncher and stands him upright before the Sioux maiden. "You talk to Red Moon about your troubles," says he with one or two nervous eye twitches. "He'll find your little brother."

"No is brother. Sister Pawnee she. Family, she family must be find." But Left Hand has went away and took Eagle Chief by the arm. Red Moon can't speak right at the present. He stares at Lark while he chews, chews some more, and holds a bulky hand over that swollened cheekbone of his. Finally the rhubard goes down in one hard gulp which makes Lark's eyes get big. She looks at the slouchy dude with his purple cheek and long loose hair. "You Pawnee is?"

He tilts his head. "Which?"

"Find to help?"

"Sorry?"

"Man say you is help."

"In what sense?"

"Sense no understand."

"Understand what? I don't understand."

"You no is Pawnee?"

"You don't speak the human language?" He throws her some sign language to try to make heads or tails but his thick hands and fingers stutter something awful.

"Sister she Pawnee!" A big breath was involved in getting that there deposition out in halfway passable grammar.

Red Moon starts pulling at one ear and saying ow and wanting to know if the gal'd ever been stung by a baldface hornet in her life and if so was it in the ear. Yeah he didn't think so, since Doc told him it's very rare. And very painful and that's why he slammed into the nearest tree. "That one." He lets go of his cheek and points. "Did you say your sister is a human being?" he says with a kinda abstracted crunch of rhubarb.

"Sister she Pawnee, yes, sister baby stole. Oglala is stole. My people is. Please." She seems as surprised as anybody by the wordiness of that outpouring.

Human being, Pawnee, same thing, that seems to be the opinion of this Red guy thinkin aloud. "Okay. I'm starting to get the drift. You're an Oglala. You can't help that, it wasn't your fault." Lark lays her hand upon her breast and nods hopefully when she hears Oglala. Then Red submits the following: her sister was a Pawnee kid who got stole and become her little sister.

"Is yes!"

"You want to find the family that your sister was snatched from."

"Is yes! Very!"

"I can't help you. I don't know why Left Hand made such a ridiculous promise." And away he limps, leaving Lark speechless in two languages, until a old woman comes up and pulls her astonished elbow in the direction of one of them earth lodges, only pint-sized. To be quite honest, the old woman could stand a few more teeth and hairs, but her tiny lodge is festooned with every feather, shell and garland known to the plains. She's smiling cavernously up at the black smoke uncoiling from the hole in her roof where a light breeze scuttles through. The little lady gestures and jabbers away comfortably to the Sioux maiden in tow. I guess when I weren't lookin maybe some of that wily smoke musta blew itself around and got into Lark's big backward-gazing eyes.

Quite a dandy sunset up the river. Warm western breeze rippling through the glossy treetops. Head rested against Old Grateful's lovely trunk and hand patting her gnarled roots while music pulses through one of them little pod thingajigs and *Black Elk Speaks* gets more dog-eared by the page. If I could take a picture I'd—

"Dad!" She sits bolt upright, her bare knees bent, and her red hair sticking up in the back hosting a lost ant or two of the same color. Brent Portillo don't seem nearly as surprised as his daughter.

"Hi, sweetheart." Over his reading glasses he glances down at his young scholar while he draws some sketches and numbers on a clipboard. "How'd it go today?"

Tanya throws her headphones on her lap. "Dad, why are you here?"

Dad ain't a bad sketcher and there's a optimism and calmness about him as he scans the woodsy riverbank. "Planning to bid on a contract, sweetheart. Drainage, grease disposal, general disposal systems."

"Don't you know what that runoff will do to this river?"

"Don't you know what this contract would mean to my business? To your future?"

"It's not worth it, Dad. You don't know how toxic this whole plan will turn out to be."

"Then do you want a shoddy job done on it, or somebody who knows what they're doing?" Dad's tone has took on a kinda beveled edge all of a sudden.

For answers, Tanya looks straight upward. O.G. looks downward. Brent Portillo looks riverward, and beyond.

The hump's the best part. Well I wouldn't know, but that's what they say. They being the folks on the plains when they serve roast buffalo for dinner. Like-minded dogs from all across the village has gathered outside the tiny lodge having whiffed those savory smoke fumes spiraling through the roof, which is the best free advertising in the world. Lark's the honored guest at the flickering lodge fire, and she don't quite know what to make of that. Her stomach, though, had run on empty and it knowed exactly what to make of such a spread.

"You have such lovely thick hair, my daughter," says Many Clouds, carefully sponging a small chunk of cornbread around the inside of her bowl.

"Thank by you, auntie." Lark's lookin at the old lady's scant gray locks. "You—. Stew of you. Best taste ever I see. What little green thing there in stew?" She points at the large clay pot over the fire.

"Beans. That one is beans. That one with the little white seeds is squash, my dear. The little yellow pieces are pumpkin. These are from last autumn, dried and stored. All grown right here in our own garden, my daughter." Tomorrow she'll take her for a spin, says Many Clouds quite tickled at the idea.

Across the fire sits Wolf Chief, crosslegged, full and content, smiling over with teeth as straight and white as the hair avalanching from his wintered head. All at once the old gent's mouth and eyes form circles, and he puts up a deep-rutted index finger. Managing, without a word, to get his legs unkinked and upright, he toddles off to a dark corner of the lodge.

"Where are you going, Old Man?" Many Clouds, you can tell, ain't expecting no answer, and she has plenty of time to explain to Lark that her husband can't hear worth a darn but he's a good old boy and they been blessed for more winters together than the fingers of five men.

"Now here's something, my child," says Wolf Chief dropping beside her short of breath, "you've never seen in your part of the world. Phew." He opens a sturdy pouch and gives Lark a generous look and smell of its contents, which is dried leaves and roots and the like in a pulverized state.

"What she?"

"She, I mean it, is the Golden Flower of our land." The old guy seems to hear every word Lark says, which is curious. "A little of this rubbed on your tummy and your worst stomach cramp is gone like a crazed antelope. Comes in handy," he says with a wry old glance at his wife, who's heard that joke before. After givin him one of them looks that wives give husbands who think they're so smart, she stands to her full four and a half foot of loft, straightens her shoulders back rather imperial and kinda fetching, somehow, in the dwindling firelight. Then she patters over to the small woodpile in the long earthen entryway, and Wolf Chief engages their young guest in a pretty passable conversation regarding the exact layout of each and every earth lodge and its function as a sacred observatory of celestial bodies that ordain much of Pawnee life. Many Clouds has just plenished the fire back to respectable height with bandy sticks and a few big buffalo chips throwed in when comes a sudden loudish thunk at the doorpost. When that fella Red Moon clumps in two seconds later rubbin his forehead, Lark's the only one that seems to think the phenomenon deserves even the least bit of interest.

Somethin about the way Red Moon says hello auntie and uncle and makes hisself at home in their lodge gets you thinkin that maybe these old folks really are his auntie and uncle. Stranger things have happened.

Ain't long before Many Clouds has served everybody with tea and Red has contrived a way to avoid the question marks and searchlights in Lark's eyes. But her tea's gettin cold and his don't seem to wanta go down without a hard swallow, and finally the young feller turns his head to Lark but leaves his eyes on the fire. "Granny might know something. I doubt it though."

"What is?"

Aunt Many Clouds knows a doomed conversation when she sees one, and she don't hesitate but to jump in and get Lark to semi-understand by means of simple words and quite a lot of pointing that her husband's dead brother's widow is Red's Granny, and Granny might or might not know something. About what it is that their guest wants to know about. Their guest don't seem to have a real clear grasp of what's being proposed. But she sure has perked up at whatever glimmer of hope seems to be reflected in the sparks that shoot and fade from this here friendly lodgefire.

First thing Granny asks, when they find her sweeping her and Red's little corner of the big lodge they share with the Blue Fox, Dance in Snow, and Hunting Dog families, is why her grandson's limping. Again.

"Nobody's limping," says Red as he turns and walks away, mouth twisted but legs steadied, with the excuse that he has watchdogs to feed at the farm. Granny brushes off her long beaded buckskin dress and pulls her platinum braids back. Then she bewails the manifest fact that her grandson's turning klutzier and klutzier with each new day. She confides to her visitor her personal theory of it: it's because of what happened that time and how the young feller's never been able to face it or talk about it. "He's haunted," says Granny Bright Eyes as she sits the Sioux maiden down on some soft skins before she starts to explain a lot of things. Patient and simple so's Lark can follow. "I'm so worried about that boy," she says. "The way he punishes himself."

Lark's a soft-breathing wood figurine with cheekbones raised just enough to squeeze a drop of pity from her eyes. Them eyes see the old gal's two palms come up with the fingers stretched her way, quavering, in an effort to straighten what nature has bent. It was that many winters ago. For a moment Granny puts the hands tight over her mouth. Then she goes on. The Oglala attacked at dawn. Their village was handsome, up on the South Loup. What can you do, you're always prepared but you got lives to live. The villagers fought their heart out, and the Pawnee heart is the bravest. But the Oglala is fierce and they was many. Pert'ner half the village got wiped out. Some young women and children was never found, and Lark's sister could of been among them that was took captive. No way to tell, really.

Granny puts her hand on her chest for a minute and blows air like as if she's cooling a spoonful of corn mush for a little hungry tot. Lark sits sunken and stares at the floor though ain't much to see this far from the lodgefire. Then Granny tells about Red Moon. When the Oglala struck, the lad was out hunting, she says. By the time he got back, well. Red's young wife and their unborn child was caught in the crossfire, and when they found her she bristled Oglala and Pawnee arrows alike, that's the sad truth. Them that was left alive just scattered. She and Red come here to Eagle Chief's village, and Red give up on hunting and scouting and warpaths and them pursuits which he wasn't exactly cut out for in the first place, and took up growing things. Which it turns out he's a dang champ at and their people admire and accept the strange fellow for the man he is.

"Still he much of sad, he look," says Lark.

"He blames himself, my child."

"Blame is?"

"He was out hunting but he got lost. That's the reason he came late."

"Lost?"

"The boy has no sense of direction." With sad diamonds for eyes, Granny wags her tongue and clucks her bowed head. Hold it. Switch em.

When Red comes through the lodge entry tryin his durndest in the firelit gloom not to favor one leg over the other, he's startled by a low rumble that seems to come from a glowing pipe. "What's the point, man?" rumbles Crouching Panther Who Speaks With Deep Voice, youngest son of Blue Fox. In the darkness it ain't too easy to get a precise reading on exactly where and which way this cool scout lurks. You can just make out the direction of his disapproving eyes.

"Who says there has to be a point?" says Red, whose eyes go in the same direction. Where he can surely see that Lark has took in the whole saga by now. And it ain't hard to guess the young gal is twiceover grieved: by what them folks has went through at the hands of her people, and by the reality that her poor sis probly don't have no close family left anywheres among the Pawnee. Does it help that Granny tells her in a choken voice that Running Water is welcome to come live with her and Red and be a beloved granddaughter to her? And hugs Lark tight and rocking like her own granny always done? Some. Some.

If there's no vacancy, why the heck don't they just turn the sign off altogether? Wouldn't that make more sense in the long run? But Lyle likes his neon, I guess I already dwelt upon that earlier.

Well, the crickets don't give a hoot about vacancies or no vacancies, they're havin themselves their usual summer symphony. They only hush up when they feel like it, or when them kids at the motel pool scream above their splashes. So four soft taps on the door don't hardly make a ripple.

Cosetti, though, has pretty sharp ears. And his tongue, well—he's just gotta open that door and make some kind of wise crack about gettin paroled early for good behavior. Only it ain't Laertes standin there in the doorway. And Cosetti don't know what to do with his battery toothbrush, he just turns it off and sticks it in the faded purple pocket of his gym shorts that say Northwestern. Them bandages bulging up beneath his undershirt, though: nothin much the feller can do to put them out of sight. In fact she's staring right at them like they're a smoking gun, so he steps back grinning and lets the news gal in.

He shuts the door, and you'd expect the regular Janet to pepper the cagey dude with about nineteen burning questions before he has a chance to offer her a chair. But this ain't the regular Janet, and she ain't been seen or heard from all day. What she says, and she says it shaking, is "I know what happened last night and I know why the cover-up. I want to hear from you how you justify in your own mind that kind of deception."

Cosetti ain't interested in justifying nothing, he wants to know what in the world is going on with her. It's personal, it doesn't matter, that's all she'll comment on the subject. "It didn't help to find out through hearsay that you could have been killed last night." Something in his eye says there may be something in her eyes that Cosetti ain't been on the receiving end of in a long, long time. She swallows. But a poor swallow.

"You better sit down." With just a slight groan, he takes his big brief-case from the green easy chair and don't seem to know what to do once she's in it. He sets on the bed and the more he looks at her and tries to pry into what ails the gal, the more pale and grim gets the gal. She's shivering in her sleeveless shirt, so he switches off the air conditioner behind her. "Janet," he says bending over her just a little with his hands on his knees, "can I get you something? A beer? I got cheese crackers—"

Well, most of it goes straight on him, and he's so stunned that it soaks in pretty good before he does anything. But, since Janet ain't eat a bite since breakfast except coffee and half a protein bar, what she spews up is mainly yellow muck, so it could be worse. Cosetti keeps saying it's okay it's okay and his hands hover over the woeful sickly heap like a maestro tellin his woodwinds to pipe down. By the time she's burped a few last sour notes and cried herself out, Steve's back from the bathroom sponged off and changed into swim trunks and company teeshirt. He hands Janet a wet motel towel to clean her face up with. Some of the color has came back.

He puts his suit jacket over her shoulders, which is still shivering, then he steps out for a second and comes back with a cold Spritzy-Up from the pop machine and pours some into a glass. Steve lets her drink it down before he starts in cross-examining her emotional nosedive since the press conference this morning. She don't want to open up. Besides, says she, he still owes her an explanation of what he was tryin to prove by digging up her old editorials and committing them to memory. "What do you want with me?" How can a fella look away from eyes like that like that?

"Mmmh—" Absent ventilation this here room ain't the freshest place on earth. I'd have to admit. With a deep flush and a smatter of sweat basted across it, Cosetti goes and slides the big window open some, then sets back down upon the bed and studies the brown crisscross stripes on the beige carpet. He musta strained that incision, some way or other, his left hand is pressed hard upon his side. His cheekbones is raised, but not from no grin, when he looks up and says "You talk to me about what's going on with you and I'll answer your twenty questions. Deal?"

His right hand hangs in the air like the wooden arm of a old abandoned railroad crossing. "Why did you have to bring him here!" If an explosion of fiery words could wallop a young fella and tumble him over like in the funny pages, Cosetti'd be on his back looking up from that motel-grade carpet with little tweety birds circling his head.

"Who?"

"He made me feel like a fool. Ugly."

"Krolak?"

"I was fine," she says, "I erased him years ago."

"Apparently you didn't, Janet," and he pours the remainder of the soda in her glass. He wonders if she don't mind him having a beer.

"I'd rather you didn't." He nods quite sympathetic. Pretty soon Cosetti's that statue they call The Thinker as Janet's eyes grow to Sandhill lakes and she ounce by ounce and drip by drip starts to heave upon this stranger all the emotional bile that's been bottled in her poor gut since—. Well, it seems she had the crush to end all crushes, back in college, for this grave character Krolak. Janet was so dismal deep in love, it seems, every time she was out with the guy she couldn't just say whatever popped in her head like a normal gal, she had to—choose—every—single—word—like—a—Pulitzer—Prize—article—or—something. One little adjective that wasn't pure Shakespeare might break the magic spell of their love. Her love, that is. No, his love. Oh, I don't know. She embeds her face in that cool white towel and appears to shake several hard truths into the warm lamplight. Cosetti's eye can just about discern them truths, if I'm any judge.

Anyways, while Krolak would just stand there stroking his beard and thinking lofty thoughts, Janet was frozen in her words and even more frozen in her actions. She had to show the brainy anthropology major how she felt about him. How to best go about that? She had not the foggiest. She vowed to heaven that Saturday night she would kiss his serious whiskered mouth. I mean really kiss him. Or die trying.

Saturday night after he walked her back to her campus apartment and they finished their coffee over a conversation so tense that all it needed was the climax music from some Betty Davis picture, she kissed him. It was a long kiss, even though she had some trouble getting her trembling lips approximately near to the dude's pale brooding ones because she first had to kick out one or two kitchen chairs that was in the way, still it was a long kiss. And he kissed her back just as long. And she kissed him and they kept that kiss going. And nothing happened. Nope. Not a darn thing. That kiss just died of old age. And so did Janet's heart.

Steve blows air out his thin nostrils and his question to her, after a minute, is how could she give up on romance because of one little flop. With an egg-headed narcissist.

"Because," she says, "what's the point?" Steve ain't following. So she has to look him in the eye: the one that ain't but a patch. Didn't he have self-doubts, she wants to know, after—

"You mean could anyone love me?" That's exactly what she means. "Never. I got engaged, married, had a kid. Got divorced. And it's not your turn yet."

"I think I'm ready for a beer," she says.

"I don't think that's such a good—"

"Trust me. I'm a journalist. But maybe you don't have any beer. Maybe that was a hoax all along."

"Oh I've got beer all right, Janet. I own the beer. Bought it outright."

She thinks that's an awful droll thing to say and says so. They uncork two beers. They neither of them was kiddin about being thirsty. "It is my turn, by the way," she says. "Let's have it."

"Mmmh. You want my confession." The regular Janet might have made a remark, but this Janet just raises her beer bottle in a little ironical salute. He ahems and don't know exactly where to start and wants a direct question put to him, being a lawyer and all I guess, so she frowns.

"Okay," she says, and she shrugs his swanky suit jacket off her bare shoulders and I sure like the nifty way she done that. "Mr. Cosetti: You came to Cottonwood because your company is so benevolent it just has to spread its largesse to all our poor downtrodden peasants." Askance is how the corporate counsel regards that there opener. Outside somewhere a couple car doors slam. The crickets trail off to a low hum. "But there's something else you're here for. From the beginning you've looked at me in a way that makes me feel—suspect."

He sees there ain't no way to duck or sidestep. "You're right," says him. "I wanted to see you. Possibly say hello to your dad."

"You know my dad?" Doubt's another word for what we wrestle with in our heads. And it's always the good and the bad squaring off, we don't know which is which half the time.

"We played golf together."

The regular Janet ain't here to comment that she'd have pegged him as more the hunting and fishing type. This one just needs to know When.

"September nineteen ninety." The spine of this Janet sits up straight. The lips fuse. "Charity golf tournament. Support the Nebraska Beef Queen Pageant. We were paired up."

"Okay." I ain't sure if Janet's heart has took a siesta.

"Twelfth hole. I was up by three. We had some good-natured chatter going on. His turn to tee off first."

Suddenly she's whiter than before she took sick and her index finger is revolving in the air like it's tryin to trace the dark iris that ought to be there, gazing at her half-amused, but ain't. "It was the tee," she says in a voice that's been strangled to a whisper.

Funny time to chuckle and grin. "No. His number two wood."

"His golf club hit you in the eye?" You ain't seen or heard true anguish if you ain't in this little motel room.

"Hit me in the gut. He had a great follow-through, your dad." Things go all frozen for a second like the old projector at the Tivoli Theatre before Milt finally got around to upgrading everything to digital. Her eyes has glued in on Steve's adam's apple tryin to make sense I guess, and her mouth is startin to form the letter W. "He lost control on the follow-through and it sailed into my belly."

"So your eye was okay."

"Just had the wind knocked out of me." Janet knows the feeling. "He felt so bad, he took me to the clubhouse and bought me a beer. Two beers. I wasn't much of a drinker at the time. He didn't know. I was buzzed, I shouldn't have driven. I never made it out of the parking lot. Ran my truck head-on into a light pole. Windshield shattered."

"Oh Steve."

"He shook my hand not a minute before I crashed up."

Her head is in her hands, saying she never knew, all's she knew was he had a breakdown. "A complete breakdown."

"I gathered," Cosetti says.

"I was at grad school, I had to step in."

"Hell of a job you've done."

"You know I'm going to have to write up that robbery."

"Your readers have a right to know, Janet."

"I think I can find some room on page thirteen between Livestock Roundup and Obituaries." First smile since—ever.

Cosetti roves his sure eye over this new face. Without saying nothing he reaches towards the desk chair where his best suit pants are throwed. Finds his handkerchief, spits where the monogram ain't, and wipes a fleck of dried puke from just about under her ear. Where the hair bends like September barley in a hailstorm. He sticks the hankie back in his suit pocket. Wadded. It wasn't that he hadn't blew his nose once or twice at that press conference anyways.

"You're sure, you're absolutely sure she was the girl in your dream?" Slowly he shakes his head at the uneasy light of his late lodgefire. Eagle Chief's mood if anything is darker than ever.

Straight across sits Left Hand smoking furiously, and not twitching no more than about every once in a while. "It's her," says the feller with his pipe-clenching smile. "To a T. I take my destiny seriously, Chief. I think you know that about me. The Great Spirit doesn't send a Morning Star dream to just anybody."

You would think there ain't nothing Eagle Chief couldn't pacify with the wisdom of his two downward motioning hands. "Why don't you wait, son, for another occasion. This girl may not be the one. It seems she came here on some sort of benevolent mission." Chief lets his eyes take stock for a minute, circling the lodge where, in the shadows of their compartments along the earthen walls, his kinfolk are pert'ner all folded in slumber. Cept his wife, though, she returns the chief's meditative glance as she sits rockin their newest grandbaby with quite a nice Pawnee lullaby and the resins of corn husk and poplar bud on a finger pressed to the child's sore gums.

A tallish middle aged gent in a great beaver pelt hat shaped like wings paces around the lodge, listening to the discussion but coming often to a standstill with narrowed eyes and thoughts, apparently, from other realms. Once in a while the gent opens a red and white painted satchel and examines various poultices and herbal concoctions.

Lefty wants to know, with a violent twitch of his eyes and nose for emphasis, since when exactly are sacred traditions no longer honored in Eagle Chief's village. He turns to the village priest sittin on his right. Secret Pipe is one of these fellers that likes to sip his tea for a while before recognizing a spiritual question, and'll wonder and stare into the heat waves high above the flames before handing out parcels of enlightenment. Finally, in a voice traveling from somewhere else, and I don't mean Topeka, the feller starts in very soft-spoken about some pretty deep things. Like how small and how humble are humanfolk in the great universe. How folks like them is born on the earth, walk upon the earth and no where else, and die right there where they lived and walked. Which brings him back again to the idea that humans is pretty puny things, in the scheme of it. "Who here can gainsay that?"

Now he ups the volume and puts that question neither blinking nor liftin his eyes off of Left Hand and it's an even bet as to which one of these shaved and feathered heads wants to win this here staring contest worse. "To find our way," and as he sips his tea he coughs just enough to forfeit the contest and dribble some on the jangling bearclaws that line his buckskin shirt. "Ahum. To find our way, do we look only at our moccasins, forever trampling and kicking dust? Is it the small stones scattered from underfoot that show us what direction we must follow?" Thus the feller turns his reverend gaze onto Eagle Chief, whose mouth starts to sag like melted wax. "Or do we look to the heavens to guide our steps? For is it not the Great Spirit who makes the stars to move? And for a holy purpose?" And then the feller brings up the timely example of the Morning Star in particular and while the decibels trickle out of his voice the awe floods into it. Hushed to a near-whisper, he prods his three listeners to think about the brave bright Morning Star and whether, those times when it's situated so as to rise up alongside the sun, that ain't a sign. A sign to be paid attention to. And what about dreams, ain't dreams supposed to mean somethin, especially dreams with stars in em? Priest sure seems to think so. Eagle Chief don't know what to do with that there gospel, which is hard stuff to argue with, except to cast a doleful set of features towards Left Hand. Whose bouncing head don't need no words to imply somethin like What'd I tell you, Chief? Am I vindicated? Lefty scoops his open hands toward Secret Pipe. As if the holy man was performing center stage at the Bijou Theatre and just finished levitating a entire Comanche war party and was takin his encore bow.

Then the priest starts to launch into one of his famous parables, which is called The Boy Who Saw A-Ti'-Us, but Lefty cuts in and reminds the pious feller that they've already heard that one a time or two, and his smile makes it pretty obvious he decided to understate things by about two or three score.

"Good Sky," says Eagle Chief to the fella who's pacing up and down, "Weigh in here, will you, my friend. What was your impression of the girl?" Just then a serious young feller with beaver hat aflapping dashes in to consult about somethin private and pressing. After a bunch of swift hand movements and excited utterings, it's awful clear there's been a unusual mishap took place somewheres hereabouts. Good Sky leans down quite calm and dictates several whispered instructions to his assistant, checks the lad's red and white satchel, then sends him on his way. He puts his hands up so as to discourage questions. The three gents seated round the fire just look at him. Well, one of them smokes and smiles.

"All right," says Eagle Chief to the medicine man, "about the girl?"

"Ah, the girl." Good Sky keeps his pacing up, but now his hands are clasped behind his back and his long frame tilts forward. "Well, let's see: the subject presents as a young adult Sioux female who is casually groomed and attired. Since this evaluator has not had the opportunity to perform a physical examination, only gross findings can be made at this time. The young princess appears to be alert and oriented as to time and place. Some agitation was noted, but this would be expected in a new tribal setting." Boy, Left Hand can roll his smoky eyes with the best of em. "Head, neck, torso and limbs are unremarkable."

"You got all that from 'hello'?" Lefty says.

"What hello?" says the doc. "I never met the girl." He run into Many Clouds after supper, is the way it come about.

"You base your opinion on what a meddling old auntie tells you?"

"No. I base my opinion on what my meddling old auntie told me. Strike meddling."

"Great Spirit help me if I ever need medical advice in this village."

"Always gotta be a skeptic in the crowd."

"The point is," sighs Eagle Chief, "the girl is basically healthy. Of course," and his glance pivots over toward the priest for a second, "you want someone healthy. But that's a two-edged knife, my friends."

"What's the problem, Chief?" says Left Hand, pipe smoke sifting through his teeth. "I know how to handle a two-edged knife. It cuts the way I want it." And with a curdling war whoop the feller leaps up and swipes his weapon at a long loop of the medicine man's hair as he paces by in abstract self-analysis. I can see Doc turning and standing there scowling and clicking his tongue but I can't hear a single click, what with the howls of a left-handed jackal who dances in the firelight, shakes a fistful of hair and knows exactly what he wants.

Friday

"*I* gotta hand it to her," says Bill McCarmady, turning the *Caterwauler* over to Milt and preparing to fit a quadrant of blueberry bran muffin to his large mouth, "she put that nonsense about the tree and that high-priced nut from California right on the front page."

"It says he's from Portland." Milt points at the dude's bearded likeness in grainy newsprint.

"I was never too good in geology," Bill says.

"Geography," Milt says, gaping.

"Don't you know when I'm messing with you, Milt?" Considering a grinning mouth full of fiber, Bill's speech ain't too sloppy. "Then, she found the human interest angle and really played it up. That squirrelly vandal comes off smelling like a rose."

"She made him into a goddam local hero," Kenny says. "She can pull all the heart strings she wants, she'll win no points with that garbage."

Bill and Milt stare across at Kenny, and Ray wants to know what his insurance agent has against kids, all of a sudden.

"I got nothin against kids, Ray. My kids." He drains his coffee and shoots a look across the diner like he's Elliot Ness staging a roundup of hoodlums.

So far, none of them four has spotted the little article about a certain attempted robbery, buried on page fourteen. Next to the fascinating news that sorghum has went up three cents since yesterday alone.

He says cut it out, and he halfway ain't foolin.

"I didn't say a word."

"I told you stop gawking at me, hot shot. One more smirk and—"

"I gotta look in the mirror, Trail Boss. It's in the drivers manual."

"Since when did you become such a stickler?"

"I've got a newfound respect for the law, you know? The law is a beautiful thing."

Cosetti tells J. Edgar Hoover to spare him the nauseating platitudes. They pull up at a medical office building, where Cosetti gets out and puts on his cowboy hat. "You're not gonna fall in love with the meter maid, now are you?"

"Cheee. That's good, Steve." The big guy loosens his narrow tie and gropes for yesterday's *Wall Street Journal* and half a bag of mustard flavor pretzels among the debris in the front seat. His boss heads leisurely for the office of Dr. Daniel Huber, Chiropractor, Acupuncture and Weight Loss. On the way he closes that little list of names he's got on his phone and calls up a certain smalltown newspaper gal and she and him trade each other a couple of Hi's. You know the kind of Hi's I'm talkin about, the kind of Hi's that—hmmmh. Well. Maybe I, maybe I shouldn't oughta really be listenin in right at this minute. You know?

Anyways, if there's anything goofier to have to sit and listen to than a sappy gal and a moony dude on the morning after they discover they was meant to be, it's two of them moony dudes and the only thing worse is if one of them dudes has to look at the other one's foolish grin in the rearview mirror of his limo all day. And snicker low enough that his boss don't hear and end up downright touchy.

"Does that hurt?"

A wide brow swivels sullenly on a thick neck.

"How about—"

"Aaaaaah!"

"—that?"

"Great Spirit Almighty, Doc. That hurts like the—oh for crying out loud, Doc, hasn't medicine advanced enough that you people don't have to ask that question any more?"

Good Sky gives his patient a patronizing nod and starts checking the strips of doeskin swathed round Red Moon's swelled knee and tellin his young assistant what a skillful job he done wrapping the limb late last night. The other leg, by the way. Not the one Red was limping on when the evening was younger. Well the junior medicine man flushes and gives large credit to the Sioux princess who'd stood by and helped him administer the first aid under the moonlight, and when he tells his mentor what a good nurse she'd make it's possible the young feller may be thinking more in terms of making babies than just delivering somebody else's.

"What exactly were you doing, Red Moon, when the trauma occurred?"

Nearby on the new-swept floor of their compartment kneels Granny, weaving a straw mat while her worried eyes pingpong between her grandson and his healer.

"Honest, Doc—I was just walking the Princess back to Wolf Chief's lodge. I was simply pointing out our corn and melon fields and explaining how we grow the best of any people in the valley. 'Possum poo!' she shouts at me out of the blue, so I tell her, look, if she doesn't agree with what I'm saying she can just say so, she doesn't have to get insulting. So she's excited, shaking her head, and jabbing her finger toward my moccasins. Well, she warned me a little late, I'd say. I stepped in it, my feet went out from under, and I twisted my knee, Doc. Remember that time with the moose who tried to run off with my prize squash? This was worse."

Good Sky closes his eyes and massages his high narrow forehead for several long moments. Then in a very flat voice he starts in advising Red Moon all the things he should and shouldn't do whilst his knee heals up. Just as he's tryin to find some new or better way of imparting to his number one patient the importance of watching where he's going at all times, the loud roar of a major dogfight reaches their ears. Good Sky strides out after his assistant, their beaver hats attempting to get airborne. Outside the two medics come abruptly upon Little Brother, that friendly scout with the scalp-studded britches, breaking up a yelping, lunging cyclone of fur. The young brave has plucked a mangled mass from the snapping jaws of the village pack. The medicine man directs the feller to lay the suffering animal in a safe spot and, with the help of his assistant, starts to gently examine the poor critter in the shadow of Wolf Chief and Many Clouds' tiny lodge.

I guess the decibels of that dog scrap was pretty high, cause even old Wolf Chief has puttered outside to investigate, and Lark has trailed her host into the morning sun. Soon as she steps into the clearing and looks round, she clutches her head and screams out a word, a simple Sioux word but it leaves me shaken to the core. Lark runs half-hysterical and falls to her knees beside the Doc. With some heartbreaking garble of Pawnee and some pitiful hand signs, she makes Good Sky savvy that this here mauled and bloody creature's her dog. Doc has Lark hold Scout's big head in her lap while he and his assistant run their hands over the fella's gouged belly and ripped shoulder.

"I'm sorry, Princess," says Good Sky as his assistant starts handing him sundry kinds of herbal mixtures and poultice fixings. "He must have been a great loving dog to follow you so far." Lark was on the verge. Doc's words has plunged her over. "Weren't you, boy?" he says, stroking the quiet head of the stricken animal. Little Brother, nearly on the verge himself, kneels and spoons a trickle of water down Scout's gashed throat. Red Moon weren't supposed to hobble out with his bad knee, but he done it, with one of his old hickory crutches. From the doorway of his lodge he leans and watches helpless. There's a score of curious children from the surrounding lodges does the same. Not that none of them tykes ain't seen animals kilt every day of their young lives.

Top floor of the City-County Center, office of the mayor *pro tem* of the Cottonwood city council. Sounds like a mouthful but the whole point is that Cottonwood ain't like a Grand Island or other big cities that need a fulltime mayor. So Cottonwood just goes and hires a guy to be city manager and run the day-to-day. Then the five city council members take turns being mayor. It's kinda democratic.

Well, after lunch Steve Cosetti is sittin up in Mayor *Pro Tem* Ted Racine's office and is being told pretty plain that he oughtn't to be there and better clear out quick before somebody gits the wrong idea. Most fellas don't grin when they're gittin throwed out of an office, but Cosetti ain't most fellas. He tells the mayor once more that he ain't there on behalf of his company whatsoever, he's wearin a different hat and he's only came there as president of the Kansas-Nebraska-Iowa Meatpackers Political Action Committee. Mayor Ted Racine don't appreciate the distinction. "That's all well and good, Mr. Cosetti," frowns his Mayorship, "but your being here in any capacity while you have unresolved petitions pending before this council is absolutely unethical and is prohibited by city bylaws. And I didn't teach Civics for thirty-five years without learning a thing or two about political ethics. This meeting never took place and you are on your way out."

"You've got a primary coming up."

"What's that got to do with you?"

"You've got a smart young stock broker running against you. A real dark horse." The incumbent starts to darken himself. "My organization may feel that your opponent happens to be someone who will be more—sympathetic, shall we say?—to our industry. Someone we can support. Generously."

Once that little hint has a chance to soak in, Mr. Mayor don't hesitate to enter a slightly outraged objection to blackmail when it's waved in his face. Above his very own desk.

Would a blackmailer wear such a personable grin? "Mr. Racine, you and I both know that political action committees are free to—"

"Mr. Cosetti, I hope I don't have to count to three."

Cosetti puts on his cowboy hat, and walks out, checking off the last name on his little memo, and then clicking delete. The Mayor *Pro Tem* slams shut his office door, and the walls shake. Them walls is thin. Can you imagine, a twenty million dollar government building with walls like wax paper? The Mayor can't hardly doodle squigglies on his official city notepad but what they can hear it in the outer office.

The little outer office ain't empty, there's some chairs, a coffee table, magazines like *Platte Valley Life* that Cosetti left open to the article called "Interstate 80: 10 Roadside Restaurants Worth the Drive." There's black and white pictures on the walls: the building under construction at different stages. Under one of them pictures rests a desk, with a computer, scanner, what have you. There's even a person at that desk, trying to do background research on various city council bills, and eat celery. But Tanya Portillo has took a little break from her research, and even her celery. With very red hair and, right at the moment, face as well, she just sets briefly and stares at her phone. Like it's the dessert menu at Jensen's Drive-in. Then one freckled hand goes to the wastebasket and comes out with this morning's *Caterwauler* and the foil seal from a Greek yogurt stuck to the sports page. Summer internships can be very educational things.

"Mom, Dad's acting weird," says Jessica Benson. In flip-flops and a wet swim suit the little towhead makes a beeline toward pasture and barn. By the time Dad's out of the pickup truck, Jessica has came back running and Dad and Mom is both acting pretty weird. Like they swallowed the canary. And Jessica wants to know where he's at. And is ready to cry. He's not in his pen. Gilligan, that is.

She ain't old enough to quite understand. "Dad's going to get you a new little calf, Jessie, to raise up just like Gilligan. Maybe one of his babies. You can win another Four-H ribbon for your scrapbook." Jessica don't want another calf. Gilligan is special. Her fiery tears prove it, til long past dinnertime.

When she calls and breaks their date and he wants to know howcome, she don't say no comment. But it dang near amounts to the same thing. Cause if she has to work late on some big news story he still don't see why they can't get together after. Talk, have a nightcap.

"No."

"Why not, Janet?"

"I'll be tired."

They'll be tired together, he says. "It'll be good."

"Not tonight, Steve."

Mmmmh. In a lonely motel room with no clues and stitches in his side that's startin in to throb, it's hard for a feller to figure out how the old Janet come back into the picture and where the new and improved Janet has suddenly went to.

I guess the big hoedown was advertised pretty good, cause pert'ner everybody in the village has showed up, dressed in their best. The shindig don't start til after sundown, so it's nice and cool and still as folks come out and spread their feast around the big council fire, the central plaza of their little colony. They shoo away the dogs, who was pacing the area and salivating long before the food showed up. Like every dance, it's the beat that gets the young people moving. The tom-tom players is startin out slow and steady, and little by little gettin up some speed and oomph, and the excitement of the crowd revs up like a old roadster. The young guys and gals hop into the firelight between the inner circle of stones and the outer circle of logs and begin their rhythmic steps, all movin clockwise, only the gals as graceful as herons and the guys like pouncing cougars. Every once't in a while, one of the elders stands up and chants out an ancient song with raised fists, and the crowd joins in til the feller grows so tired and happy that he has to set down and let his wife revive him by fresh venison and tea.

Now, a dramatic moment and a catchy name are not things to waste. So when Left Hand, flanked by his best scouts, makes his entrance, he carries his trophy lance in the vice-like appendage suggested by his name and stirs the crowd to a odd mixture of reactions. He stands quite satisfied, fer a minute, like Grand Marshall at the Rose Parade. Then, with a couple rolling twitches from his eyes to his nose and back, Lefty walks into the circle of young Pawnees, which opens for him, and joins the gyration. Ain't a bad hoofer, have to admit. Could work on his posture and his timing just a bit.

While them young folks that's so inclined is dancing, Hill Seeker, that fierce oversized dude who is Left Hand's steady right hand, he keeps himself occupied by parading around the circle with Lefty's trophy lance held high. But every little while the big feller gets bored, so it seems, and for amusement he likes to come up to an unsuspecting brave, raise the deadly lance in a powerful hand and execute a sudden feint of striking to the heart. When, as most usually happens, the unfortunate dupe flinches even just barely, Hill Seeker will howl and whoop like a pack of coyotes bringing down a antelope. You can't say, in truth, that the feller ain't got a sense of humor, afterall. But it sure is an off-brand of humor, ain't it? From the pulsing dance circle Left Hand gets a kick every time his big sergeant pulls this witty stunt. Eagle Chief, from his sharp-eyed vantage among the chanting elders, don't seem to fully appreciate the hilarity of this charming horseplay.

Well anyhow, speakin of food, there's plenty of savories spread out by each family for them and their neighbors to feast on throughout the evening. But some of the more colorfuller and temptinger dishes is only now just arriving. Granny Bright Eyes squeezes through and finds a spot for her special potato, pumpkin and bean stew and for herself to set down beside and dish out to anyone with a bowl, plate or whatever receptacle. Some boys and girls from Granny's lodge has followed her with more pots to set down, and last comes Red Moon tottering upon his crutch and hunched over with the weight of a great caldron tied round his neck. A pretty good cluster of villagers has soon lined up to sample what Red growed in his garden and Granny perfected over her fire. Little Brother is first in line, acts like he ain't eat in days, and Granny's tickled as anything.

As out of the way as he can git, Red Moon stands and from time to time overhauls his face, which is glum when he rubs his sprained knee or his purple cheek, glummer when he gazes at the ecstatic dancers, but not-quite-so-glum when he chances to look over at his Granny. As he leans on his crutch and regards the old woman dishing out food and beaming bigger with every helping, Red don't seem to notice a huge shadow coming and looming up over him. Nor the shadow slowly raising a monstrous arm. All at once a driven lancehead plunges to within inches of Red's heart. Red don't flinch, just frowns. "At some point in time, Cousin, you might want to think seriously about growing up. Some jokes wear thin after so many moons. And weren't that funny to begin with."

Hill Seeker chuckles and marches on, shouldering Lefty's trophy lance. Strangely enough, Red Moon follows exactly behind the other fella, sideways and stumbling, wailing in pain and swinging his crutch wildly at the air. Don't seem likely but I'll be danged if the big prankster hasn't accidentally snagged a bundle of Red's long hair around that lancehead before he shouldered the ornery weapon. Since Hill Seeker tends to be a sorta oblivious dude most of the time, and since the good villagers can't but gape in wonder at this weird and spooky firelight spectacle, Red ends up gettin himself yanked and dragged nearly full circle before anyone figgers out the poor boy needs help. Granny knowed somethin was wrong but she's went pale and fell back on her thin elbows and folks is fanning her and making her take a bit of her own soup.

"Freeze!" shouts Doc Good Sky as he jumps in front of Hill Seeker and grasps the dude hard by the shoulders. "What is the motivation for this odd behavior? Do you understand the implications of such deviant acts of denial in inappropriate social situations?" While Hill Seeker is still working on the word "motivation," Doc's assistant hands him a scalpel-like knife and he swiftly frees Red's tangled mane. The two medical men help the shaken lad limp to Granny's side, where they bathe the old gal's forehead with a mistletoe balm to revive and comfort her before they start checkin out throbbing knees, burning scalp and so forth and so on across the beleaguered battlefield of Red's sad body.

Now, the midway point of Red's painful spectacle happened to of been the moment when Lark Laying Eggs up and joined the party, along with old Wolf Chief and Aunt Many Clouds. By golly, don't she look glamorous. With flowers and feathers, a new dress and all kinds of fancy doodads. Lark don't look bad either. In fact, when the distracted crowd realizes the Sioux maiden is present and been sat in a special reserved spot, nothing but shushing and rubbernecking is heard and seen. The tom-toms cease, dancers halt in their tracks, children playing tag tag theirselves, and chewers of roast buffalo swallow what ain't been completely chewed. Lark's been anointed pert'ner head to toe with a murky red dye, and decked out swanky in a kinda sacred black gown and robe. If she decided to blush, or flush with anger or confusion, you'd never tell the difference.

Well, in no more'n the fleeting spark of a firefly, this here jubilant party has became a still-life painting. Until at last there is movement. It is Left Hand. The lean warrior goes up to Hill Seeker and resumes possession of his trophy lance. Thus equipped, he goes and stands before Lark, breathing hard and smiling at a arm's distance. The feller bows and she ain't whatcha-call flattered by the salute. Lefty don't pick up on stuff like that. He'd rather speechify. "You are quite radiant, Evening Star. How can anyone say that the Great Spirit hasn't brought you here in answer to the sacred Morning Star dream? My morning star dream. My destiny. This is all for you," he says with a broad sweep of his lance at the whole gathering. The whole gathering obviously sees itself being indicated, but it don't seem to be quite on the same page as Left Hand. It seems to be more on the page of whispers, shrugs and significant looks. "I have a gift for you, Evening Star," says Lefty, whose deep-voice comrade the Crouching Panther steps from the crowd and extends to Lark a pretty ritzy jacket sewn of shiny otter pelt, with some of the little heads still attached.

"Thank of you," as she shakes her head in protest. "No is for me this big celebrate. Me is far place from, new in Pawnee land. No want special this. Just want my brave dog. Now he bury at river. Doctor try so hard, but too much sick." Her eyes is nigh to flood-level. "Thank of you, Doctor." Still kneeled at Red Moon's side, Good Sky looks pretty watery himself. Lark turns her lips in and, with the back of her hand, covers them and seems to search for answers to all this sorrow in her empty lap.

Left Hand has his mouth half-open to contradict his reluctant Evening Star, but he can't get no further than that. The reason is that folks at one end of the circle has erupted into hysteria and something big and steam-driven as a locomotive has thundered into the village and scattered everyone in its path. The thing comes to a full stop not ten feet from the circle fire.

I think I mentioned some time ago that buffalo is skittish critters. I'm thinkin this here bull buffalo, massive and forbidding on the exterior, probly got hisself detached from his herd, then spooked by a dog and run in a blind panic smack dab into Eagle Chief's village. Frightened as a wild colt, snorting and stamping his hooves, the bull's dark eyes shift into the high alert that only terror can invoke as he finds hisself in the middle of his worst nightmare.

Once the folks see that the awful brute is stationary and considerably more stricken than theirselves, they calm down and a reverent hush settles upon the village. Secret Pipe smooths his feathers and gazes into some far off corner of oblivion, then with hands raised takes two or three priestly steps in the beast's direction. He starts speaking in a low even voice and pretty soon he's got the animal's eyes locked with his as if they was on magnets. Everyone's riveted and rooted to the spot. Well not quite.

There's a foot planted forward. A long lance is drawn back over a left shoulder, and a smile grows hard between urgent twitches. A lean set of muscles flex like a catapult released, but a grunt turns into a gasp and that lance goes nowhere. Around Lefty's wrist are Eagle Chief's granite fingers, and there they stay until the warrior drops the weapon and smiles at all the folks as if the whole thing was just a clever act. There's part of his smile that lingers on Lark, though, and that part tells the maiden that he meant every bit of it. Every bit of it all.

Now that Secret Pipe has the lost bison kinda tranquilized and do-cilized, he kneels down right before the beast with a wave of his arms and head that tells the entire crowd to do likewise. He then leads the village in a earnest prayer of tribute to the wide-eyed beast and all of his kind for the blessings they bring to the Pawnee, who depend on the buffalo for pert'ner everything. Well, there might be one fella that don't look quite so earnest or humble as the rest of the folk. Anyways, pretty soon that buffalo turns and trots out the way he come, and he goes with good wishes and prayers.

Different story entirely if they should ever meet on the prairie during huntin season.

Saturday

*Y*ou ever feel outa sorts and crotchety of a morning? Somethin rumbly and gassy in the pit of you?

Sure, I got faultlines like everybody else, it ain't just out west in California that gets shook up once in a while. But that ain't it, exactly. This here's a pretty dawn. The Morning Star has just now rose up above the spreading sunrise. Spring has near about blossomed out everywhere she oughta blossomed out. Only something's gnawing down below, eatin at my inner crust. Just a little tense, that's all. Off kilter? Some of my latitudes is chafing my longitudes.

"I like this whole game, man. This is more fun than shooting timber wolves on the run." A sharp elbow into his comrade's ribs—upper ribs—and a pair of big flexing shoulders emphasize this remark. Them shoulders is about level with a sea of shaved heads. Make that a river. The particular shaved head attached to the shoulders is a foot above. "I'm thinking that I might get a Morning Star dream like yours. You don't think so, huh? I'll dream up a girl twice as pretty. I'm thinking maybe harvest time. I got nothing scheduled. Heh."

"You don't dream."

"I could if I wanted to," says Hill Seeker with an expression that even warpaint could not do justice.

"You sleep like the dead." Behind a shifty cloud of pipe smoke lurks Left Hand's signature smile.

"Then I'll dream when I'm awake. You got something to say against that, Cousin?"

"You don't choose, my naïve friend. They choose. If the Gods need a dreamer, they decide who. If the Great Spirit looked down and appointed me for greatness, I had nothing to do with it. Got that? Who am I to raise my hand and question his choice? Eh?"

"What's naïve?"

I'll be danged if pert'ner most of them men and boys that sung or danced last night ain't already gathered, spruced and spiffed, and is marching out of the village in a long column. Some fellas is singing a sacred song. Crouching Panther's the entire bass section. The procession is led by Secret Pipe in his swellest robes, feathers, and sacred trappings. In the midst is Left Hand, wearing warpaint and a ancient costume from the sacred bundle of the village. Alongside and occasionally batting at branches overhead with Lefty's trophy lance is Hill Seeker. The squirrels seen him coming, they ain't no dopes. Old Wolf Chief, with Lark takin regular slow strides to match her host's bitty steps, sings in his hoarse dry voice. Whole different tune than the one that echoes among the men but it sorta blends, in a bluesy way. Lark's bedecked in last night's black robe, this time with black moccasins to match, her right half painted red and her left half dyed black. Upon her thicket of hair is a headdress of black-tipped eagle feathers spread out like a fan. Over the sacred robe she's wearin the otter jacket Lefty proffered.

"Oh, my daughter," says Aunt Many Clouds, the only other gal in the procession, "you look so beautiful, just like a—ulp—" By golly the kind lady has suddenly choke up, with her lip and few teeth gone aquiver and one hand upon her scant hairline as though she's suddenly grew dizzy.

"Please Auntie, no sad be. You is mess up pretty face paint we spend long time to making before breakfast eat." Yup, coupla brave tears has already streaked the red and purple paint which decorates Many Clouds' round cheeks and brow. She ain't blew her nose properly, neither. But I kinda like it drippy. Anyhow, in my opinion the gal don't need no paint to enhance what nature has generously give her. "No is so bad, Auntie. Nobody say but Lark know she soon be marry to Left Hand, he show it very important thing for he, important for Pawnee people all. Lark no understand this, but Great Spirit understand and Lark trust." Auntie can't hold back no more and Lark pats the lady's chubby wrist that's wet with wiped tears. "Still I spend happy day with Auntie. Only nighttime be by Left Hand. Much he be no home, far he go hunting, fighting." Near enough to overhear these broken Pawnee words walks Eagle Chief with his eyes groundward and pressed with so much sad and sorry wisdom that a person can't help but wish that there was more fellas like him in this harebrained world. Longside the Chief are Good Sky and his assistant, beaver hats drooping and looking very lost without their medicine satchels.

Over a little rise and across a small creek hemmed with willows goes the bushy path. Lark flings a couple hasty glances over at the young squash and beanfields along the right side of the path. She perks up at the song of the meadowlark, and the fluttery flight of pheasants from a cornfield, but there ain't nobody there. Just a snoring dog with dreams of nibbling upon little rabbits and five or six little rabbits nibbling upon the tiny radishes they like to dream of when they snore away the long prairie winters. Ain't nothin perky in the brave face Lark turns to Auntie. After that the strong backs of the marching Pawnee is all Lark seems to see.

Paths sometimes make sharp turns. This one has did just that. Smack into the dense growth along the wide river. Some fellas hold the twangy branches for the fellas behind, some let em snap back without no second thoughts about whose eyes or nose might get whapped. Eagle Chief and the elders take care that no branches snap back upon Lark, nor Wolf Chief nor Auntie as they grope forward. Then the column breaks through into a shady clearing. And upon a very odd sight. Yet familiar. Yet odd.

What's familiar is them two tall trees: cottonwood on the south, elm on the north. About yea apart. With coupla arrows in the ground as markers. That Red Moon had wanted to take an axe to day before yesterday. Before Lefty showed up with his pretty prize.

What's odd is them two trees is now the uprights for a sturdy platform of fresh timber crosslaid between. Various cured skins enclose the makeshift stage. Why, the big trees is painted one red one black, and the platform's snazzy with bunches of white downy feathers. Lark at least has that to marvel about. Little Brother jumps forth from the assembled crowd to help Lark mount the platform, which is not so easy in the heavy black robe. "You're awfully brave, Princess. Great Spirit, you know, the Great Spirit'll—um." He swallows.

"No be worry. Soon Lark be Pawnee. Lark Little Brother cousins be." Little Brother's lower jaw plummets, along with his heart, no doubt.

Once Lark's deposited up on the platform Lefty hands his smoldering pipe off and approaches. But Lark ain't focused at the relentless dude, she's searching the gallery of faces, painted or plain, don't seem she's found what she's looking for.

"Pawnee chiefs, warriors, old men," commences Secret Pipe, facing the assembly from a little dirt mound at the base of the stage, "I have this night followed the sacred journey of the Morning Star." The priest points to the east sky just visible peeking through the trees. "The Morning Star," looks at Lefty, "has called to the Evening Star," motions toward Lark. "You two have been chosen. You shall purify the earth to make it bountiful and rich. Our people are grateful beyond the power of words. Begin." He tilts back his head and intones a pretty fiery chant, which is took up by many of the fellas in the audience and meanwhile, Lefty ascends to the north end of the stage and stands before Lark with arms crossed.

So, Lark's a wistful actress on the stage, waiting for something that perhaps don't exactly match up to the script she had writ of her future life and the kind of fella she had halfway figured to spend it with. When Secret Pipe calls a full halt to that there chanting, and turns to face the platform, nobody ain't talking, nor whispering, nor moving, nor hardly swallowing. This clearing is so peaceful you can hear the gentle rustle of the leaves in the elm tree above. Which is funny, come to think, cause there really ain't no—. Hmmmh.

I don't suppose Lark's been briefed on much of anything of how this here ceremony is to proceed. Up here on these fresh-laid trunks of willow and box elder the gal's pretty nigh turned hardwood herself. Her eyes don't, but many other eyes do, seem to watch Left Hand's agile namesake slowly slither around to his back, leaving the right arm crossed where it was. He opens that back hand and grasps the sacred bow and arrow that's deftly put there by the Crouching Panther who has stole up to the stage like a shadow. In one neat nifty move, and with a shrill war cry joined by several of his troops, Left Hand draws back the arrow point blank at Lark's heart, which has altogether quit pumping if her pallor is any gauge. Eagle Chief, deep amid his people, must have somethin on the back of his rust-like hand that needs some careful inspecting at the moment. Auntie Many Clouds has took a unusual interest in a small stitch on the side of her dress. Them two fingers on that bowstring is twitching with readiness to let loose that uninvited arrow.

"Nobody's sacrificing anybody," cries the elm tree. Exactly a split second later a solid object geronimos down from the tree and wipes out any sign of Lefty. And his bow and arrow.

While the spectators look up in awe, Red scrambles to his half-crippled feet, scratched, dusty and speckled with bird doo, just in time to catch Lark in a violent swoon. Maybe this young feller's not such a total klutz as was generally believed.

Ain't it lucky that Good Sky's young assistant was the sprint champion of the village three corn festivals in a row, and I think them beaver flaps give him lift. When he gits here with his and Doc's satchels, Red Moon is still hollaring at everybody.

"If you're bent on spilling innocent blood, cousins, you'll—you'll hafta spill mine first. Does everybody get that? Raise your hand if you don't! Oh," says the lad, holding his broad head. "I think I made myself woozy." The young farmer really sincerely wants to know, in a voice that's now angled downward and subdued: who started this tale that you need the blood of a virgin sacrificed to the Morning Star to guarantee good crops for the Pawnee? "It isn't so, it can't be," and he looks up and around at the villagers. "You know I've proved it time and again." At his feet sits Lark, with Auntie's dear arm about her and smoothin the young gal's hair with soft nubby fingers. The shiny otter jacket has been took off Lark, and with hands folded in her lap she's prayin I think from Sioux Lookout or somewheres and not here on a Pawnee scaffold built for sacrifice.

With the rising sun stretching through the tree trunks, Eagle Chief stands among his warriors and nods his head slow. "Red Moon," he says, "your heart is the heart of a lone eagle. And, in a sense, your eyes are the eyes of an eagle. Not unlike the Great Spirit, you see things from far above: how small and foolish are our ways. Son," he adds, "if you could just put down that rusty hatchet you're twirling there before you—Thanks." He speaks for a spell while Red drops his hatchet and catches his breath. It's like the Chief is thinkin out loud, and some other shrugging elders chip in as well, and the gist of it seems to be that, maybe, though traditions is what keeps the Pawnee people great, even the Pawnee ain't necessarily perfect and perhaps there's a tradition or two that oughta be rethunk.

Left Hand ain't quite conscious yet, his face is froze in a permanent twitch and the big shadow of Hill Seeker leans over him like a dim cloud in a windless sky. Doc and his assistant is both busy tryin to bind up Lefty's tongue where a slice got chomped off when he was leveled mid-aim, in the act of claiming his destiny. Left Hand won't be speaking at this here meeting.

"Grateful For What?"

By Brandon Sorenson
Age 15, Cottonwood High

What good are old trees?
How silly they are.
They're no more to me
than the moon or a star.
They might shade my house,
but I live at the mall.
Don't you love how the stores
have new clothes in the fall?
While in autumn a cottonwood's
just a polluter
of leaves on my car
and my thousand buck scooter.
What this town really needs
are more restaurants and stores.
I like my steak medium rare.
How about yours?
When trees stand in the way
of American progress,
which side would you
rather be on?
Take a wild guess.

Well, Ray is tickled like I ain't ever seen Ray tickled before as his coffee cools and he reads out loud Brandon's poem that's the grand winner of the *Caterwauler's* essay contest. Then he reads what's written under the winning photo, which by golly is Keith's debunked tree carving snapshot. Well, says the caption, doesn't this picture speak volumes, and isn't this, deep down, the most poignant image of all the fine entries received? Ray smiles a tired smile so warm and so even that Nickano Jr. might pop it in his display case with the buttery crescents. Kenny's smile, on the other hand—nevermind, that ain't Kenny's fault, only it does go pretty good with how he can sit there and scoff at poems and pictures by young overachievers. "Again with the kids?" says Ray, who's been around Milt so much he's startin to talk like him.

Kenny don't get why everyone's so critical of a little meatpacking plant, and says so. His bewildered hands and face appeal across the vinyl booth for some enlightenment. But enlightenment from Bill or Milt is generally suspended during critical muffin or pastry maneuvers, which are currently in full sway. "Is everything so dandy here, Ray, nothing should ever change? God forbid we should molest a single blade of grass to try to make things better."

"Did you read this article?" Ray wants to know. "He tried to buy the city council, lock, stock and barrel. That company oughta be tossed out on its greasy fanny."

"He didn't try to buy anyone, he just lobbied, the way they lobby in Washington."

"Thank you," says Ray. "I rest my case."

Kenny throws his hands in the air and then, with a cry of pain, finds out that probly wasn't the best thing to do with a shoulder that ain't halfway healed. Well that puts a lid on all the rancoring, and the booth's a battleground no more. At least until Monday. Bill has took part of the paper from Ray, and Milt has took part of that from Bill, and it's pretty tranquil by the time Bill gets curious to know when Milt is heading to the big barbeque.

"At three," says Milt, "or whenever Estelle gets out of the hairdressers. Why, you want to carpool?" He winks at Ray.

"Not if you're driving." Four coffee mugs take turns getting a sip or two emptier. News items rustle in occasional gusts of page-turning. "I wouldn't mind getting there early, though, meet some of those Omaha people. They can't run an operation like that without some local banking."

"When you get there, look for me, Bill," says Kenny. "I'll introduce you." I guess he does turn a little bit pink when his three coffeemates sit up straight and stare. A pink-faced Kenny could mean so many different things.

As you might imagine, a sacrificial lamb that finds itself spared at the last second will pert'ner always scamper off without no formal leave nor polite chitchat. And keep a anxious lookout for hands that instinct says are bent on needless bloodshed. Well, whether foolhardy or fearless, this little lamb don't scamper so much as ten modest paces. In fact, while that scaffold gets took apart log by log and Red Moon lets himself topple under a maple tree, this little lamb diligently tends to the feller's ailments both old and new and tidies up his impressive inventory of bandages, dressings, and splints. Bold and meteoric but a short while ago, the young farmer does his darnedest to avoid eye contact and any subject other than the many varieties of eagle corn and their proper fertilization. Though, when that racy topic gets exhausted, he does attempt a piteous smile and tries an old joke out on her, the one about the Kiowa priest who turned his first wife into a flying squirrel and, well you know how it is, unless you're born and raised Pawnee you ain't gonna quite get the subtle innuendo of such high-brow humor.

When the last remnants of the scaffold is gone, the stately cottonwood and elm are unburdened and them arrow markers is stomped deep in the ground, they find themselves left alone in the clearing. Lark hands Red his crutch and they creep back to the path they come by. Bein a planter and all, Red can't skirt the pumpkin field and not stop to yank out at least a dozen or so thirsty weeds, but each weed seems harder and harder to pull and needs closer and longer study until the last weed just sits in Red's palm like he ain't ever seen one before. Or, like he's sorry he pulled the sucker out. Lark, arms slung at her side kinda like a yanked-out weed herself, can't do nothin but watch. Wait. And deeply shiver. "You is pain feel?"

His is one a them faces that don't hide much, so no matter how the lad rallies his battered body to stand straight and make motion look easy, before he's back upon the path his face has betrayed him outright. The path itself is narrow. Two folks face to face don't leave much room to breathe. Nor evade. "I'll come back later and spread some buffalo—"

"If no you danger jump, I be die! Why you do this danger? Why you tell chiefs must no kill Lark? Maybe they is kill you!"

"I doubt it." With but one shoulder can Red Moon shrug. "We need to get you home, Princess, you're probably—"

"I no princess."

"I no prince."

Ah, the sight of that there smile. I don't know when we've seen the likes of it since she run off in the first place. And we don't see it for long now neither because all too soon it's smothered with a shy hand. "In village my people," and a moment's pause has brung a distant look to Lark's eyes, "I think man who save life girl, they is marry! Great Spirit say truly they is marry."

"Oh," says Red. I don't believe, and I've seen a lot of folks, but I don't believe I have ever seen a head take that long to complete a single nod. "Sounds vaguely—. In the vaguest sense it—. I, I think we have the same tradition. Heh."

"Tradition! Yes, good tradition."

Why, by golly it is a pretty sound and reasonable tradition, the young feller agrees wholehearted, and demands of the listening bluejays and poplars to know how anyone can expect folks to break too many traditions in one day. Heck, if they're married, they're married. That's how Red tries to condense it, and bright-eyed and nodding she seems to savvy that concept pretty good. He puts out a hand. Hers ain't overly coy. And I'll be danged if they ain't a pretty swell fit. Wrote on their faces is the question where do we go next. While that riddle percolates, she aims to make sure that the fella's fully acquainted with the genuine name that she's called by in her tongue and what it means and how it happened that the day she was born they saw this bird in a nest and—

"I know, Lark. I get it." Not much doubt that he also knows he's got himself a real corker.

"Granny say name by you Moon Red."

"Red Moon."

"Same. Name sound sweet to me. Lark sing for Moon Red in sky. Moon Red smile on Lark for happy sing." A real corker.

Anyways, to be on the safe side, Red lopes into the village and rounds up Granny and Secret Pipe for a hasty blessing upon their two callow heads. And then by golly, on a day of frisky windblown clouds playin hide-the-ball with the Sun, them two young folks take the path that winds down toward the river.

Well, naturally, Lark and Red have a pretty nice time of it down by the river. And this very evening, a wispy cottonwood seed embedded in Lark's thick hair since the night she run off comes free and floats away. And catches in just the right cranny of riverbank. Where it takes root. And where three hundred fifty years later we know her as Old Grateful.

Say, I guess I might mention while I'm at it: another tiny seed gets planted this mild evening. She will be known as Silver Leaf, the great-great great-great—uh, I believe you're gonna need to tack on another twelve greats—grandmother of Tanya Portillo. Yessir.

Gilligan's wire pen sits under a tall sycamore. The old tree helps shade the back of the bandstand that's smack in the middle of the park. Pawnee Park is shady, green and flat, but only because a hundred forty years ago the collapsed earth lodges was leveled out and planted over. Once plentiful, Pawnee artifacts is rare to find these days and most folks has stopped looking. Just E.M. Tinker, mostly, and he's got a pretty groovy collection at the Historical Society.

Gilligan ain't eat or slept, all the big fella wants to do is stand there snuffing air out his snout, and now and then jab his great horns at the air and kick those sharp hooves into the warm afternoon grass. Them eyes of his is big as a fifty cent piece and them nostrils like two trumpets. Just like they get anytime he would hear the word "steer" pop up in conversation around the farm. Or anything that sounds like steer: stair, stir, star. If you was a bull, you wouldn't much relish the implication of that there word, either.

The Bensons decided they better skip the Euphemion company barbeque. Only Gilligan has RSVP'd to this one.

"Horsie, horsie," says Lorna pointing a tiny finger upwards from the Smold's double stroller.

"No, Lornie," says Allie Smold, "that's a cow."

"That's a cow, Mommy," says Liza. From his pen Gilligan looks at the twins like maybe they're a new kind of Jessica and maybe he don't need to shiver with fear quite so much as he's been ever since they come and loaded him in that truck yesterday when Jessica was at swimming lessons.

"Girls, what do you think of the cow? Is he big?" Two curly heads gape and barely nod.

"Bull," says Kenny, as he winks and walks over to the wide tent where the Euphemion folks is camped out.

"Bull," says Lorna as her mama smiles at her daddy's narrow shoulders growing narrower.

"Fascinatin-rhythm-you've-got-me-on-the-go," wails the Cottonwood High Jazz Band. "Fascinatin-rhythm-I'm-all-aquiver." Bang, boom, clash and thunk goes Nickano III on drums. Somewhere back in the tent where coffee and sweets is being served, Nickano Jr. adds his own cookware percussion.

"What you see is what you get, my dear," says Milt sipping his coffee, as he splits his funnel cake and gives Estelle the smaller half.

"You're mean," says Estelle, who's been trying to lose twenty pounds for nineteen years. "And Flip Wilson you're not."

"Milt, my man," says Galen Nicolette of the *Cat*, taking a giant step forward but leaving one foot in the line for roasted corn-on-the-cob, "I've got some great ideas for fall ads I wanna show ya."

"Let's get through our summer clearance first," says Milt. "Check with me after the Fourth."

"The fifth it is," says Galen, retracting his step and glancing at the open mouth of the little Camp Fire Girl behind him in line.

"I'm glad she's over there and not here," says Brent Portillo while he mustards and onions a hot dog and burger from the Grouse Club's smoky braziers. "She'd see all this meat and start griping and pouting."

"I wish she'd just have stayed home," says Mrs. Portillo looking toward the west end of the park, where sounds of protest echo through the treetops from the parking lot of James Fenimore Cooper Elementary School.

"No cutting in Cottonwood," hollers Tanya Portillo with a waving sign that says Euphemion Keep Out.

"No cutting in Cottonwood," holler the local chapters of the Arbor Lodge Society. The Anti-Cruelty League. The WHADUI's, which is the We Hate DUI's. The members of the Holy Day Church which is strict vegetarians. The punk rockers from the High School. And any members of the PTA who ain't got a personal financial interest contrariwise.

"No cutting in Cottonwood," hollers Dr. Chowdhury in a squeaky timbre and proudly rattling his sign which says Cottonwood, Not Cottonwouldn't.

"Trees, Not Tenderloins," says the T-shirts of all these protesters, with a picture of a cow tied to a cottonwood and a chain saw aimed at its neck.

"Pete, any thoughts on what effects a meatpacking plant would have on Cottonwood?" says Peg Rossiter for the *Cat* to a fella wearing an Astros cap and shelling peanuts.

"It's about time," says Pete. "We need more jobs. And the next thing we need is a nuclear reactor to run it with and cut our electric bills."

"You have a good day," says Peg pretending to write those thoughts down in her notebook and raising her eyebrows at her boyfriend Lance who installs solar.

"Do you have Tahiti water?" says Deputy Gillespie where bottled drinks are being handed out.

"No," says the Euphemion worker who processes Edible Byproducts at the Concord plant and eyes the little patrolman kinda suspicious, "but I have Target."

"With thprinklth," says Cory Gillespie, the hawkeyed deputy's little boy, at the ice crème booth. "Thankth."

"Lord, help her see the light," says Deputy Banacek shaking a wide moist brow at the sight of his boss and his least favorite wide receiver sharing a lemonade. Same straw.

"How's the Crusade going, Banacek?" says Deputy Anderson walking by much amused. "The infidels winning?"

"With you as their Grand Potentate, Anderson, God only knows," says the large blond knight.

"No problem," says Reeves Palmer when Ray and Babette Stidwell ask him to please send some Chamber of Commerce water bottles to the hot protesters, which include their daughter who teaches yoga over at Hastings.

"No Water...No Slaughter. No Water...No Slaughter," chant the protesters when they refuse to accept any handout from meatpacking sympathizers.

"I'll take one," says Keith O'Conner, who's on probation and daresn't get closer than curbside to the protest itself but opens the bottle and pours it out with dramatic flourish while his mom looks on horrified.

"Sorry, Mr. Palmer," says Brandon Sorenson with a cringe when his frisbee conks the chamber chairman and knocks his Event Staff cap into a recycling bin.

"Huh?" says old Sid Haabert who's busy looting the bin of cans and bottles for his own personal recycling program.

"Nah, don't worry about it," says Reeves. "Just move your game over to the baseball field, huh guys?"

"Nice move, Brandon," yell Brandon's friends. "Hey Brandon, how about writing a poem about your killer frisbee. They'll put it in *Sports Illustrated*."

"How about trying to catch a frisbee for the first time in your life, Schellmeyer," yells Brandon with a deep flush and a Herculean heave over all their snickering heads.

"Let me just—" says Kelly Waligorski after Sid comes up to her information table and stares at her can of Dr. Pop until she guzzles what she can and surrenders the five cent article with a deep hiccup and even deeper dimples.

"Looooove-for-sale," warbles the lead trombone doing a standup solo with eyes closed and nearly parting the spiky hair of the lead saxophone with her slide. "Appetising-young-loooove-for-sale."

Nary a word says Bill McCarmady, away from the crowd behind Gilligan's pen as he tenders three personal checks of five digits each, made out to K.N.I.M.P.A.C.

Nary a word say his two big rancher clients standing alongside looking like they just figured out a way to rustle cattle without leaving no tracks.

Nary a word says Steve Cosetti as he grins and sticks the checks in the lining of his fancy cowboy hat.

Nary a word says Gilligan, who's so dang fascinated by these cowpoke fellers on the other side of the wire that his tail forgets about swatting away them tenacious flies that came for the greasy food but like cattle on the hoof almost as well.

"I didn't expect to see you here," says Steve Cosetti on his way to the bandstand.

"Is there anything you want to state for the record?" says Janet, fumbling with her wallet. "Here, you wanna see my press credentials?"

"Not necessary," says Steve, putting up his hands. "You have a right to be here. And I know you think I'm scum. Hey, I've never been called PAC-man before."

"So you're ready to confess to political extortion?" says Janet but her two eyes don't quite hold their own against his one. "I didn't think so," says she, and walks away.

"Can you move over that way a little?" says the Riverside TV reporter to the KOTT radio newsman as they wrap up coverage of the protest and set up in front of the bandstand.

"This far enough?" says the KOTT newsman, moving two centimeters and flashing a devilish smile and eyebrow lift at his buddy the *Cat* photographer.

"Cameras are setting up," says Cosetti's blonder intern tossing her long hair down then back, like them models do under them bright lights when they know their photographers is shooting about eighty shots a minute.

"Cool," says her chum with braces sparkling clean in the sun since timing is everything and the warm hot dog she just stuck in her fanny pack was almost but not quite bit into yet.

"Good people of Cottonwood," says Steve Cosetti from the bandstand microphone as he starts his welcome speech a shade too homespun and says how proud he is, how optimistic he is and all the other things he is about being here in the beautiful City of Cottonwood and how his company has growed from pert'ner nothing to one of the major players of the meatpacking industry which is a almost $200 billion a year industry and the largest agricultural sector and how Euphemion got where it is by innovations such as continuous-flow overhead conveyors that can hoist a live steer at the plant entrance and have choice cuts of beef in the freezer in the time it takes to drink a cup of coffee.

"No," says Beverly the *Cat* receptionist, sipping a Diet Peppy Cola and not paying no heed to the speeches, "that can't be. Look at him holding hands with his wife right this second."

"It's true, honey," says Florene with a face that could clinch the annual poker title, "Ellen Ackerman is his dental hygienist. She was in this morning for a pair of beige open-toed pumps."

"What makes her so sure?" says Beverly.

"Nitrous," says Florene, picking her restless grandson off his chair and sitting him on her lap.

"And he spilled the beans, just like that?" says Beverly. "That he's in love with his twenty-eight year old niece?"

"Mmm-hhh," says Florene with nods of pure calm, smoothing the little feller's hair.

"That's crazy," says Beverly. "The girl lives in Phoenix."

"Uuuuh," says Florene, as her head leaves off moving in any direction whatsoever.

"Our success," says Steve Cosetti, "will be your success. Our growth will be your growth. That's our platform. We want to partner up with all you folks and make the kind of future we all hope for for our kids and grandkids. I promise you this: We're not going anywhere, we're here to stay. At Euphemion we don't just invest in the community. We get involved in the community."

"That's code," says Peg Rossiter to Lance her boyfriend, "for 'we give large campaign contributions to local politicians who vote our way'."

"More thprinklth thith time," says little Cory Gillespie.

"Hey, Kirby," says Florene, on her way to the food tents, "how're those sandals treatin you? Where's Glenda hiding out at? Candace, that trip to Yellowstone must of agreed with you, you dropped at least a dress size, sweetie. Better keep an eye on her, Lou. This is my little grandson from Holdrege. Isn't he a doll? I've gotta find cotton candy pretty soon or I'm in deep doo-doo. Janet?"

"Thank you all for coming out," says Steve Cosetti. "Now let's get this party started!"

"You bet! Let's do this! Right on! Hell yes!" says the crowd aclapping, whooping, whistling.

"What's the deal with you, honey? You look like mush warmed over," says Florene.

"I'm great, totally great," says Janet.

"Uh-huh," says Florene.

"He-ain't-much-to-look-at," twangs the songstress of the country band with knees that bounce this way and that and make a short skirt and tall boots do the same, "nor-to-listen-to-nor-smell. He-ain't-the-brightest-penny, in-a-shallow-wishing-well."

"That's their smash hit," says Wendy Healy through cupped hands. "It's called 'Guess I Could Do Worse At That'."

"Catchy," says Laertes with about as much tease as Sheriff Wendy's got in her hairdo.

"Hey you big sissy," says Sean Blake, crouched and full of monkey business under the sycamore tree.

"Stupid ox," says Jordan Clayfield full of attitude and rattling the wire frame.

"Snort", "snuff" and "rumble" says Gilligan, craning his broad neck to try and see what's going on back there.

"How do you like that?" says Sean poking the pointy end of his empty cotton candy holder through the wires.

"What's the matter, you dumb piece of lard?" says Jordan ramming a fallen branch at the big feller's most private and sensitive spot. "Whatcha gonna do about it?"

"You boys get away from that bull!" says Steve Cosetti walking fast.

"Oh," says Janet with her pen frozen at "propagan."

"Mmmmoooooo," goes Gilligan's dry throat.

"Smash, Splat" goes Gilligan's pen.

"Thunder" go four raging hooves.

"Ow! Aaaaah! Gasp! Yelp!" go many human throats.

"Now!" say moms and dads yanking their kids.

"That way!" say guys hauling their gals by the waist.

"Help me!" say older folks on legs that can't run.

"He went to get ice crème," says Cory Gillespie's older sister.

"Up here!" says folks that's clumb upon the bandstand and is pulling others to safety.

"Roll that camera," says the Riverside TV reporter.

"You roll it!" says the cameraman, running toward the porta potties.

"Crack, crack, crack, crack and crack," go sheriff's rifles.

"Oh my God," say regular folks and protesters alike.

"Wail," go many children under the age of four.

"Wail," goes the fire engines and paramedics almost before the smoke clears.

"Wail," they go again minutes later on the way to the Good Samaritan Hospital.

"This good food shouldn't go to waste," says Reeves Palmer during total silence tryin to snap the folks that's came back out of their shock.

"Whatta we do with the—" say the Event Staff and folks that's pitched in.

"Let's do what we planned," says Reeves.

Feet. Backside. Feet. Backside. Feet. That's it, I can't look at it no more. Makes me dizzy, anyways. What's the use? I don't think Gilligan's Ma and Pa would of wanted to see their son end up this way. Not that they ended up any better, with a one way trip to Riverside. Can't hardly believe that thing there is Gilligan the pet bull. Though, if you don't gander too long or too close, you could almost imagine that's old Gilligan just holding on to that skewer for dear life so as not to fall into a thick bed of redhot hickory. Hard to ignore the smell, though, ain't it? I don't think I hear no lip-smacking, I'll say that.

What I don't like is the warm damp feel under the sycamore. I don't know whose is whose. Whether from two-footed folks or four-footed, it soaks in just as sure. It still leaves me dank and darkly stained.

Sunday

Sunrises in my Platte Valley can be pert'ner as handsome as the sunsets, but they never do get the same appreciation. Mornings is a busy hurried time. Red Moon has went to raid granny's cache for some corn cakes, nuts and dried berries, and Lark has yet to look downriver at the bright orange and pinks that drain into the horizon. The new bride kneels and splashes cold river water on her face and neck, fixin herself up for her hubby. A sudden shadow passes over and, startled, she blinks her wetted eyes and smiles at a cloud of sandhill cranes seeking to breakfast somewheres hereabouts. A piece of easy driftwood comes and pokes the riverbank, then does a spin or two on its back while considering whether this spot might do or does the current have choicer locations to show it downstream. Lark plucks the wood from the river, turns it in her hand and digs the thing in the air like a farmer digs in soil. No. With a little proud shake of the head and wrinkle of the nose she flings the stick out over the nearest sandbar and into the main channel. As she washes her hands and pats her cheeks once again, another big shadow falls on Lark and when she looks around that same sharp gasp sucks into her as when she was bit by that rattler. "Lean Wolf!"

"Good," says the feller with the snow-capped smile, plucking the string of his powerful bow, "you're washed and ready. If we leave now we can make Mud Creek by—"

"You better get away from here now," she says, having stood and pulled her hair back hard. "If they find you they'll—" Probly better that she didn't try to follow that unpleasant train of thought no further. Her husband will be back soon, she adds but she don't quite seem to know what consequence to attach to that general announcement either.

"Whatever this little stunt was, Lark, it's over." The young hunter straightens and adjusts the quiver of arrows slung across his bare chest. "There's a pair of black moccasins over there. They're yours, I take it. Put them on and let's go."

"If you wonder why I ran away, you just answered it perfectly, Lean Wolf."

"What kind of man would I be if I just walk away and leave you here?"

Weren't that intended to be one of them rhetorical questions? Even so, she's awful ready with an answer, to wit: the kind who's not afraid to admit other people have feelings. Or to stand up to the crowd. Hmmmh.

"A woman's judgment. Not mine. Nor your father's." Oh boy, she don't appreciate that, and lets loose a flurry of abuse on her father for what he done to her sister, and it's quite a snowstorm before Lean Wolf can impart the fact that Running Water's marriage to Rain Bear got postponed when Lark run away. Lark's eyes open big and for a minute she's adrift. "Where's Scout?" he says, looking around. He watches the gal shudder and close her eyes. "I picked up his trail. Sometimes beside your tracks, sometimes apart." She points west toward the fresh grave just a short ways up the riverbank. "It was his time," says Lean Wolf.

"Why are you doing this?" she says.

"These are not your people." He lifts his hand toward her Pawnee dress. "You look ridiculous."

"Nice to see you too."

A very chipper fella was Red Moon til he come through them trees and run headlong into a invisible brick wall. Who is this stranger talkin a low Siouan dialect to his wife is the detail he's probly sorta curious to know. "Your brother, Hon?" His satchel of food drops to the ground.

"Oh Moon Red. I tell he go, he don't go."

"What'd he say?" says Lean Wolf. "What'd you say?"

"He's my husband, what do you think he said?"

"This lumpy bumpkin is your husband? This is the mighty Pawnee?" She frowns at Lean Wolf.

"What'd he say?" says Red Moon.

"He say want know what you say."

"What'd he say?" says Lean Wolf.

"He said—" But then she shakes her head and tells the muddy river she's not doing this, it's enough already. "Stop!" she says twice, bilingual, each time with a unyielding hand toward a disgruntled fella. She goes puts her hands on Red's shoulders and they talk low. Then, with his big arm around her snug and steady, they face the other fella and by no uncertain terms she tells him he's got to hightail it back to Oglala country cause she ain't never leavin her husband nor his people.

That's fine, cept the other fella says he can't help that, he's still not leaving empty-handed. They don't know what to do but they return to the village with Lean Wolf at their heels and before too many curious villagers can gather they acquaint Eagle Chief with the situation. Which leads to a immediate confab at the big fire circle with no fire but a rising sun.

"You're a meddlesome boy," says Eagle Chief to the Sioux gatecrasher. "But, you showed incredible courage to challenge the Pawnee single-handed. You won't be harmed here."

"What'd he say?" says Lean Wolf.

"He says they won't hurt you," says Lark. "As long as you go peacefully, preferably now."

"Tell him I'm not leaving without you."

"Yes you are."

"I'll fight the whole crummy village," he says, putting his hand on his knife, at which several of the assembled Pawnee do the same. "Great Sioux warriors always die in battle. Tell him."

"I'm not telling him that. You're more stubborn than my father."

"Three days I walked."

"Then that's how many days it'll take you to get home."

"Yes, but not alone. Tell him."

Eagle Chief and the elders is becoming a bit fidgety. "Kalp him, kalp him!" yelps Left Hand from the rear of the conclave with his swaddled tongue and purpled face sticking out. "He'b kalp uth ip he hab thhe thhance!" Eagle Chief nods and a couple younger elders gently usher Lefty back to his lodge. Doc Good Sky also strolls thataway, musing and ferreting about in his satchel where he always stashes a herbal sedative or two.

She looks the Chief direct in the eye. "He say, he say—" All at once her head pivots, she wheels about and she's talkin to Lean Wolf and tellin him she'll be ready, they can leave before lunch, she ain't got hardly nothin to pack.

"What'd you just tell him?" says Red Moon to his bride.

"I know how is my people," says she. "If no he return my village in three, four day, they is send biggest war party. Is maybe be big war, most worse war Sioux on Pawnee." A dismal scowl Red Moon has, more than ready. But a proper rebuttal to that thesis he don't have. "If Lark go now, tell Oglala she marry to good Pawnee man, maybe, maybe can make long peace for you people, my people, all be friends." Nor that dissertation neither. In fact a pretty fair number of gray Pawnee heads is nodding at one another.

Poor Red ain't in the frame of mind to nod to nothin, he says okay he'll go along with her and the Sioux fella on this here good will tour. If that's what it takes. Well, she borrows one of his banged-up hands, puts it to her heart, and softly tells her mate how wonderful brave he is. But, really, that's not such a swift idea, dear, is what she needs him to understand right now. She can't guarantee what kind of a reception he'd get from the Oglala. They're not quite as open-minded as the Pawnee. And she does a little eyebrow curl toward Lean Wolf, who waits with hands on hips, by way of example.

"What if I decide to follow you?" and that don't sound much like Red's voice cause there's one of them swallows in the throat that ought to a been swallowed by now but Red's on the spot. No doubt he hates to gulp it down in front of everybody and prove what a shaky bowl of mush he's became. So when he finally does swallow, it's a whopper.

"No follow," says Lark with blinks of pity. "Moon Red be fast lost. All hill look same." But in a low murmur she promises she'll parley with her Pop and his chiefs until they say okay to having a Pawnee son-in-law. And she ratifies that promise with a warm clasp of his head against her cheek. Then she'll return and tow Running Water alongside to boot. Red's lips is mouthing something, close into his bride's ear, but there ain't no sound, just emptiness, in it.

"What'd he say?" says Lean Wolf. "What'd you say?"

The look she gives the intruder might of been enough to scare away most critters that roam the plain. Even the hungry ones.

"Could that be spelled some other way?" When Connie Griff smiles, it's not bright and happy like Lyle's big neon sign at the Best Midwestern. But it's the kind of smile that only certain ladies have. The kind that just makes you feel so good. Special. Loved and understood. Lyle must be one of the most loved and understood husbands in the region.

Not that they know of, says the farm family looking over the front desk at Connie's smile and her hospital volunteer smock.

"You wouldn't know the last four digits of his Social Security number?" According to the slight action of their heads, they wouldn't. "You're sure he was admitted and wasn't discharged?"

"Bleeding ulcer," says the wife.

"Why don't you folks check with admitting. Just through there and down the hall. They can help you."

The family turns in the direction Connie points with the little kid whining and yanking the mom's arm toward the vending machines. "Say," says the husband, "you might try Terry Gilbert instead of Gilbert Terry. He's got one of those names, you know."

"Bingo," says Connie, and I think her smile just made the man's day. "Room two fifteen east. Here are your stickers. Right up those elevators. Hey, Janet. You haven't slept."

"Have you got a ward for that, Connie? I'm willing to be committed. So what's going on here?"

"Yesterday was a madhouse. Today things are under control. A dozen or more people came in from the park with everything from nosebleed to—you name it. I wasn't here, we were seeing Lyle, Jr., off to his third deployment. But Dr. Chowdhury says it was total mayhem at the barbeque. What's-his-name your photographer sure got a great shot of you dragging Florene with her little grandson up the jungle gym."

"I didn't want to print it, but I was outvoted. And Florene's mad because it's mostly her rear end."

"So you're here for an official hospital statement? I'll see if anybody's—"

"No, nothing official. Just to visit someone on three west."

Before she gets to the elevator, but not before her visitor sticker has already fell off her shirt, Janet gets hailed by a couple coming out of the gift shop. Barb and Bob Clayfield are loaded with balloons, candy, puzzles, magazines. Janet don't look thrilled but says hey, guys. And asks how he's doing.

"Broken collarbone," says Bob. "Where he got trampled. Missed his vitals, could have been worse. Appreciate the way you wrote it up. Very charitable."

"Jordan feels awfully bad about what happened," says Barb. "There will be consequences. Grounded for a month." Janet don't say nothing. "He won't be hanging around that Blake boy anymore. It's so easy to go along when the other boys come up with these ideas, you know. And all he got was a concussion. He didn't even have to be admitted overnight."

Bob shifts his packages and his feet and says that Jordan's got to realize all the expense and trouble he's put them through. Not to mention the embarrassment.

"And the worry," says Barb. "But I guess we were kids once too, huh Janet? You remember how we were at that age. That time we stuffed gym socks into our bras and—well it was a long time ago."

"Which room is he in, Barb? I'll stop by a little later."

While Barb and Bob and Janet are waiting at the elevator, Janet looks over her shoulder at the picture of Dr. Spivak who delivered her, in the row of pictures that's got all the retired Chiefs of Staff of the hospital goin way back. Then she looks at the big patchwork quilt above the pictures and each patch has a fancy design with a heart and was made by a schoolkid. Then she looks at the grand piano by the window that nobody's ever figured out why it's there.

On three her friends go east and she goes west. She keeps goin til she comes to room 325. Laertes is messin with the little TV suspended on a movable arm from the ceiling over the hospital bed. He's got the PGA golf match on, but turned pretty soft. "You got company, Trail Boss," says he with a sorry look at Janet in the doorway.

"Come in," says Cosetti, kinda hoarse. "Have a seat. Awfully nice of you to come," he says rubbing his jaw that could stand a shave. "I'm at a slight disadvantage. Whose company do I have the pleasure of?"

She's alooking to Laertes like she needs a prompt, but a beatup shrug is all the big guy can signal back to her. "It's me, Steve."

In the time it takes for the fourth round leader to single-putt the first green and wave at the crowd, Cosetti's mouth, which is pert'ner all you can see of his face, moves not a hair. Then he licks his lips and fingers his bandages and his swanky red eye patch like they might of fell off since the new nurse come on duty. "Did you find a chair?" She just stands, shivers and nods. You know how cold them hospital rooms is kept. "Did you get any of that kettle corn?" he says. "I never could resist that stuff."

I never knew sticky carnival treats to be such a sad subject to Janet, but it sure takes her a bit to find her tongue. Which gives Laertes a chance to put a chair for her at bedside and excuse himself. "You've got some lovely flowers over there." Now she's the one with dry chops.

"I can smell them. Heightened senses, you know. To compensate."

"Don't."

"No, it's—not a problem. I guess, Janet, if I were about to be barbequed for Saturday dinner, I wouldn't mind goring a few of my enemies while I still had the chance. I just wish he'd have picked my bad eye instead. Then, I'd be no worse off than I was. No harm no foul."

She stares at this man that has become a major drain on the world's supply of medical tape over the last four days, and tries to just breathe. "You're really not bitter."

"Luckiest guy in the world, Janet. Look who came to see me. And I'm sitting here talking to."

For a second she's looking away and out the window straight down big Platte Avenue that ends right here where it runs smack into the Good Samaritan. And blinking up a storm. She asks him if she can do anything for him. "There must be something."

"Mmmmh. How about reading me your latest editorial. It's around here someplace. I wanna hear how it sounds when it's your voice. Then we can watch a little golf."

About the time the sun has rose to where it angles straight through the smokehole of his lodge and lights up the sacred bundle in its sacred place like a Chinese lantern, Secret Pipe kneels and offers a prayer for those setting out on important journeys. Outside the village pert'ner most of the Pawnee has came to bid farewells and, while they was at it perhaps, check on how a particular young farmer is holdin up. Them two Sioux travelers, northwest bound, is already a good ways up the valley, slowly mounting the northern ridge that holds back the crests and troughs of endless sandhills. Slowly, because weighed down by various parcels and pouches with the best of Auntie's larder and Good Sky's holistics. As the climbers scramble over the valley's lip they meet the West Wind, and a sheet of long black hair flapping and pointing straight back at that farmer is all there is to be seen of them two. Then, not even that.

"She'll be back, Cousin," says Little Brother, clasping Red by the shoulder, "before the corn is this high." Red's hands ply a wooden hoe among his vegetables but he may as well be sleepwalkin beneath the stars. The villagers stare but soon turn back to their lodges, pangs of self-consciousness no doubt. When Red finally drops his hoe to follow Little Brother homeward, he trips and tumbles over the old watch dog, neither one particularly fazed by the experience.

From across the field Granny shakes her head quite hopeless. There's new life all around her grandson in this familiar spot, but: you can't sing a prairie turnip to sleep or tuck it in with a kiss.

Monday

*S*ome of the staff is at their work desks on the sides. Around the long concave dais the five council members' places above their nameplates is vacant. Until Laura Ryder comes in and sets her Stucko Fasteners coffee mug down on the polished walnut where the official agenda awaits her. Then goes out again shivering. That was that.

It's 10:06, this thing was supposed to get off the ground at ten, what's the holdup? The public's packed into the council chamber, abuzz with static electricity. One way or the other. Positive or negative. Where are them council folks?

Mayor *Pro Tem* Ted Racine and Gus Peters the lawyer enter from the back in serious conversation about something until they both shrug their shoulders and take their seats and start to shuffle papers and write notes and stare into space quite frequently and the mayor goes over and starts to chat with the assistant city planner and Gus Peters gets to joking with the city attorney and Laura Ryder comes back with a sweater over her small back and Dr. Daniel Huber comes in with that leading man hair of his and plainly itching to raise one of them shoulders where the suit is let out and still bulges and wave at everybody in the gallery but he don't and Laura Ryder gets up to say hi to a friend in the audience and finally Ann Palmer scoots in and takes her seat who I'm pretty sure would much sooner be over at her flower shop primping primroses and who avoids eye contact with her frowning husband in the front row closest to her and at last they're all five settled in their places like one of them plastic toys with the little silver balls you gotta tilt just right until all five is in their slot.

Mayor Ted Racine adjusts his microphone. Back of the mayor sits Tanya Portillo with a mound of papers and doing stuff on a computer. She's wearing the exact same dress-up clothes she wore graduation night. "Good morning. I'll call the regular meeting of the Cottonwood City Council of June 21, 2010 in session. I want to thank you all for coming out on this overcast Monday morning. We have a busy agenda today, and as you can see, a very full house, so we'll get started." The public has simmered down pretty good and is watching the proceedings like a courtroom drama. "Please rise for the Pledge of Allegiance." Most of these folks actually remember the words. Even Milt Minsky, who stashes his semi-gnawed bearclaw back into the bag and covers it with the *Caterwauler* when he stands for the Pledge.

"Very good. We're first going to take up some shorter and perhaps less momentous, shall we say, business before we get to the matter that I know most of you have come here to show your concern regarding. Could I have roll call, please."

The city clerk calls council member Huber.

"Here."

"Council member Palmer."

"Here."

"Council member Peters."

"Present."

"Council member Ryder."

"Here."

"Mayor *Pro Tem* Racine."

"Here. Could I have approval of the minutes please for June seven?" Moved. Seconded. Five ayes, no nays. Carries. "First item?" The Mayor's looking over at the clerk, who forgot she has a microphone. "Coats? Oh, goats. Yes, uh, Mr. Brummel, I think you have a report for us."

With pert'ner no inflection the city engineer leans close to his microphone and reports, "Annual brush clearance by goats has completed, and they have left our city. We'll need a re-authorization for next year, if the council is so disposed."

"I just want to say," says Laura Ryder, who has beautiful big teeth when she smiles. "Everyone in my neighborhood was very pleased with the goats. And it was very pleasant to look out the window in the morning and see the goats grazing so happy and peaceful. So, job well done."

"Of course," says Dr. Huber lifting his eyes to the public gallery, "Council member Ryder lives upwind of those goats. Some of us live directly downwind." That brings little microphony chuckles from the city council folks and I spose they are a bit more tickled by stuff like that than the public folks. These city council meetings is always more or less of a love fest. At least that's what you see reflected on the surface.

"Any further discussion?" says the mayor, pointing his bushy eyebrows and eyeglasses left and right at his fellow legislators. "Any motions?"

"I move that we vote to re-authorize the contract to bring in goats for annual brush clearance for fiscal year two thousand eleven."

"Thank you, Council member Ryder. Is there a second?" Seconded. Roll call. Carries unanimously. With that old business off the table, the council is ready to hear the biweekly reports of the city manager, city attorney, community service reps of the fire department and sheriff's department, and the library manager. I'll tell ya—these folks is all top notch. Smart, professional, equal to anything you'd see in Lincoln, Omaha, or any big city. I kid you not.

Special kudos from the council to the fire department for their quick response to that suspicious mobile home fire of undetermined origin, and for their successful open house tour at the fire station. Even bigger kudos from the council to the sheriff's department for yesterday's bust of a notorious meth lab, a daring operation which is still being mopped up as they speak. The mayor holds up today's *Caterwauler* with its giant headline "SHERIFF: WE GOT THE FRICKIN BUMS!" And in the second row next to Cosetti's two interns the half of Kenny's lip that does most of his smiling for him has a kind of swagger. Somebody starts a groundswell of applause through the chamber. Mighta been Bill McCarmady in the third row, next to Milt.

"All right," says Mayor Racine after a couple of special use permits is heard and voted on, and one or two budget items is tabled. He sits up straighter in his seat and adjusts his microphone. "I think we're ready to begin the hearing on Zoning Petition seventeen and Council Motion One Eighty-eight to permit Euphemion Packing Company to construct and operate a meatpacking facility on a location that will require removal of our ancient stand of cottonwoods." The public sits up straighter in their seats and adjusts their breathing. And their faces. "Procedurally, we will try to alternate pro and con. Time constraints dictate that not everyone who wishes to speak will have a chance to speak. But I trust that you all understand that we will do our best to insure as full, fair and open a discussion as possible. Thank you in advance for your patience and cooperation. Okay."

The mayor looks down at his paperwork and then calls up the first speaker which of course would be the petitioner.

The man, a grayer-headed and less grinny fella than Cosetti, introduces hisself to the council as Maurice Benman, Executive Vice President of Strategy and New Ventures at Euphemion Packing Company, exactly as the mayor read off the speaker card. "I am very happy to be here," he says spreading his notes on the podium, "to present our petition to the City of Cottonwood. And I appreciate your allowing me to substitute, at the last minute, for our general counsel." Well, the fella goes on to expound upon all the good stuff about his company and its plans here in Cottonwood. And then he sets about deflecting any kind of bad notions that might be brought up: how they ain't going to hire no more illegals nor anybody with a criminal record of any kind, and they got systems planned to save the environment and plant cottonwoods, and health insurance and social programs for the workers, you name it they got it. And they're aiming to grow with Cottonwood and partner up in all the future greatness that can be imagined. I think this feller has probly spoke once or twice somewhere or other on similar themes, cause he seems to know how to put the main ideas together and get em across in pretty good style.

Council member Peters wants to know what he means by Employee Life Satisfaction Initiative. Well, this Benman describes all of ELSI's perks and amenities and services so pretty, I'm dang close to raising my hand and signing on right this second myself. I'd need a hand, though.

When there's no more questions Mr. Benman retakes his seat on the other side of Cosetti's interns, and the next speaker comes up, which is the former mayor of Riverside. "Mr. Mayor, council members." The gentleman has to twist upwards on the microphone just a speck, though his posture's quite hunched as he stands there under the bright recessed lighting with as serious a set of features as the morning has yet produced. "Some of you know me, some of you don't, but I'm sorry to say that I was mayor of Riverside, Nebraska, ten years ago when we welcomed Euphemion Packing Company with open arms. Before that, Riverside was a prosperous town, a good place to live, raise your family, good schools. But we wanted more. We got more all right." Pointing skywards his thumb, and then fingers one by one, he counts off stuff like school overcrowding, a drain on public health services, groundwater contamination, DUI's, crime, gangs, and neighborhood blight. He gives examples. Make your blood curdle. Worse than the nightly news.

Sittin alongside Bill and Milt in the third row, Ray gives Babette's little hand a brave squeeze. And tries his dangdest not to yawn any more than can't be helped.

The questions from the council are mainly whether, like this guy Benman just promised, Euphemion mayn't have learnt a lesson or two in Riverside and them other cities that will make things altogether different this time around. Well, the ex-mayor professes very little faith that such promises would really hold up, based on everything he's seen of corporate behavior in his career. Hmmmh.

The only person in the room perhaps capable of lifting everybody's spirits at this moment is announced, and the Chamber of Commerce Executive Director don't really have to try or say anything very original to lighten the mood. Just her being there. In all her perfectness. Why all of a sudden am I seeing Kelly with pom-poms down on the sidelines at the big homecoming game?

"Thank you, Ms. Waligorski," says Dr. Huber after Kelly's five minute spiel which has more numbers than it has words, and himself the epitome of everybody's homecoming king and starting quarterback. "Those population growth and area income projections are very impressive. I'm impressed. But has the chamber study accounted for any of the adverse side-effects, you know, that our last speaker has witnessed, personally, in Riverside? The things we've all been hearing about, or reading about, you know, whenever one of these plants opens up?" Well the chamber forecast is based on tangibles, not intangibles, and Kelly feels there are so many unknown factors both ways that would distort the economic theory of growth and investment. And as she says this and fields a couple more questions, you could almost forget about crime and pollution and start to think that the real debate here is over the relative depth of dimples. Some would vote left, others admire the right. Independents might go either way on the dimple question. But as Kelly gets thanked for her presentation, looks like there might be a council split on what she actually said and not just the way she looked when she said it: three to two, is where it stands, in favor of bunched lips over pleasant satisfied smiles.

"Dr. E.M. Tinker."

"This is not about jobs," says the retired history professor without any formal salutation after he comes down and clutches at the podium with two shaky hands, "or home prices or safety or beauty or even about history. This is about something deeper. This is about identity." Professor Tinker happens to believe that small towns have identities. Or at least used to, he says. He happens to think that children need a sense of that identity—something they might not get in big cities. He's became convinced, over time, that there's a qualitative difference between young folks that grow up in smaller communities and them that's reared in the big cities. Whether it's trees, security, tranquility, what have you, it all adds up to one thing: a sense of who we are, where we belong. A sense of self. That's his theory. And then he sits down.

Well, the owner of one of the feed and grain distributors speaks in favor. The president of the Sandhill Cranes Conservancy speaks against. The Catholic priest speaks in favor. The Presbyterian minister speaks against. A couple kids from the Future Cattlemen Club at the high school speak in favor. Two teens from the Earth and Arbor Day Committee speak against. Monique Todd from Todd's Liquor Store speaks in favor.

"Our last speaker card is Harriet Curtis." A short lady, pretty well up in years, wearing one of them protester T-shirts comes down from the back two rows which is filled with T-shirt wearers. That Theraflow stuff that she was desperate for last Wednesday night at the supermarket must of done her a whale of good. Mrs. Curtis looks robust and rosy today and her throat don't hardly croak as she starts to tell the city council how she and many others feels about the things that is happening today in the world and how it used to be in the old days and everything is changing so fast, and boy plenty of folks in this gallery is nodding though they know it don't have a whole lot to do with the actual petition before the Council. "Yes," says Mrs. Curtis, "it's so important to victimize those who cannot speak up for themselves. We need to victimize the plants and trees, we need to victimize all the animals, and of course we must victimize the children." Her eyes appeal to the council with all the compassion of her venerable years.

Mayor Racine puts his head down and rubs his forehead. "Mrs. Curtis," says Gus Peters in a voice a person might use if they wanna wake somebody from a nap without making them jump, "victimize means to deliberately persecute or treat unfairly."

"Oh," says the lady turning pale and looking so stricken she might have to go back on Theraflow. "I didn't know that. I'll sit down." Gus Peters opens his hands but don't seem to know what else he can speak into his microphone that will undo what's been did. Nevermind, the two last rows welcome Mrs. Curtis back like a hero.

"Mr. Benman," says the Mayor, "would Euphemion like the last word, by way of rebuttal?"

They would. In fact, they think they have answers to every legitimate concern that has been raised. Because they don't take these concerns lightly, let them be perfectly clear about this. And because their managers and employees have to live in the community just like everyone else. And they start to give well-constructed examples on every bone of contention. But the Mayor's eyes has slit up and his head has poked forward on his neck.

"Mr. Cosetti." The mayor ain't the only one agape in the direction of the public entrance to the council chamber. "Mr. Cosetti, my goodness. On behalf of the city council I want to say how very sorry we are for your—injury."

"Nothing to be sorry for, Mr. Racine," says Cosetti leaning on Laertes' arm. "I'm just glad to be here." By the sound of it the feller left half of his voice in the hospital, and the half that's here is coming through a strainer. Laertes sticks a open water bottle into Cosetti's free hand and the barrister swallows some, enough to slake some of that parchedness.

"Well, you're certainly welcome." Brent Portillo gets up, and then everybody in his row starts to move down a couple empty seats to make room. "Please," says the Mayor, "have a seat, Mr. Cosetti. Your colleague was just—"

"I was hoping to say a couple words myself. If Mr. Norris could just steer me to the podium." Laertes looks like a offensive coordinator watching his third string halfback run the wrong way down the field.

"Well, I don't know Mr. Cosetti, are you sure you're—"

"Just a couple words, Mayor." The council all trade funny looks with their hands turned up, and their heads afflicted with a rare palsy. Laertes cuts toward the sidelines once his boss is within a football's length of the podium. Benman surrenders the outpost peaceably, but perplexably. When he seen his fellow honcho this morning the dude was eating hospital eggs with a spoon. Cosetti gropes around in the air above the podium. That wiry little microphone can be dang elusive, if it wants to.

Sittin right there in the front aisle seat next to Rossiter, Janet flinches. And flinches. Like part of her wants to spring up and help the dude with his struggle. But she don't, being primarily froze and stuck to her seat cushion. "The thing is," and with that there little wire finally in his grasp, whether out of order or not he's got the floor, "the thing is, if I were a resident of Cottonwood with a fondness for trees, I'd file for an injunction so fast it would be signed and sealed before they figure out which end of the courthouse is up. My friends, the language is right there in your own city charter. But that's a moot point," he says. What he really come down here to say is, there's a young person in this community—and he don't know if that young man is present or not—who loves this town and those old trees so much he was willing to hurt the thing he loved to save it from destruction. "I don't condone it," says Cosetti. "But at least what the kid did was motivated by some higher moral purpose. And god help us, it shows how much those old trees mean to people around here. Go figure."

While Tanya cries at her little desk behind the mayor, Cosetti halts for a moment to swig water and mess with his eye patch. Then, like he's taking inventory of his face, he feels with both hands all around his bandages. Not that there's anything he can do about them. Now you gotta look close but plenty of these folks watching has gradually took on that burning squintiness of the eyes: the one that means they're thinkin real hard what it must be like to actually be the poor cuss underneath those dreadful bandages. Then some will realize they better abandon that particular trail of thought before they get to the point they have to put their head between their legs and do deep breathing. And then there's a few always thinking See, Mom, I told you I wasn't cut out for medical school.

Cosetti himself on the other hand admits he done one of the lowest things a person could do: tried to subvert the democratic system, and not for any honorable cause, but for selfish interests. "I'm not asking for anyone to forgive me, it was unforgivable. All I ask is for this council to think about that young man and all the other young people who will inherit whatever legacy this town sees fit to leave them. It's not that, uh—"

You know: gray is probly not Cosetti's best color, come to think of it. Even though what you can see of his face is not real extensive at the moment, the color just ain't all that becoming. "I probably shouldn't have eaten those sausages," he says, with a brave little grin just before turning back the way he come and taking one large groping step.

Now, he's right about the sausages. And by the same token would be just as right about the eggs, the fruit cup, and the biscuit with gravy.

The dude woulda had no way of knowing that Janet just had that suit pressed on Friday. $7.50 at Dew-Rite Cleaners.

I guess Kenny Smold don't care for the aroma nor the commotion. He's threw Cosetti's business card with the private cell phone number on the back upon the carpet. When he exits from the swanky first floor rotunda of the Cottonwood City-County Center, he don't hold the door for nobody. But then, there ain't nobody to hold it for anyways.

Tuesday

*W*arren R. Kessler may be a little distracted. Okay, a little more than usual. Spring is unofficially gone and Summer's not far off, so Florene's got her veteran shoe salesman trimming the front display windows. But a feller's got to look out at the world once in a while. So, while he gathers up the white espadrilles that was big at Easter and arranges the swanky pink and peach numbers that will be big sellers for June weddings, it's understandable he might stop for a minute to look across the street when Deputy Banacek stoutly pulls over a '96 Dodge Neon with loud mariachi music and expired registration. Likewise, I suppose, when strangers in dark suits happen to walk by the store he might take a short curious break from pulling out the black wingtips for Spring grads and substituting the latest in beach sandals for folks's July getaways. The First Methodist Church is but a block away, and when the organist who was taught well by old Mrs. Van Druten starts rehearsing one of them sweet melodies, you can't fault Warren if he ain't in a huge hurry to take down the various flower and rainbow motif stuff and put up all the trimmings about sun and baseball and road trips. Music tends to seize Warren by the shoulders and enchant him in far and foggy daydreams.

Out on the streets it's still slippery wet from that pre-dawn rain that come unannounced across the sandhills. Which, besides lookin pretty, means the glare off the pavement can be pert'ner blinding, each time the sun comes out from them bumpy clouds. Unless you're headed due west it's dang hard for even local folks to drive, let alone all these folks with outatown license plates or rental cars. Sheriff's deputies is out full force in dark sunglasses, raking in the revenues and always especially watchful around Todd's Liquor Store and other such purveyors. The city treasurer might be happy, but these deputies ain't, particularly today when they wish they could of gotten leave to get over to the church. Sheriff Healy even up and cancelled Tuesday morning briefing. Yup, daily briefings now.

SSI check in hand—left hand since the right hand has vodka—old Sid Haabert waits in line. Lately the lines have growed, but nobody complains, least of all Monique Todd who could of put in another cash register but: why would she? Sid himself don't really have to worry about gettin pulled over on his way home. As you know, it's just a hop, skip and jump and he likes to stretch his legs in this direction as often as possible. Plus he ain't drove in fourteen years when his license got yanked for busting down the stucco arch of the Marble Arch Mobile Home Park.

The ankle, which is a nice ankle by the way, turns this way, and that way. And this way. And that way. "I guess it's dressy enough. Or not?"

"You could still wear it to work, honey." Florene, with her face stuck in its dormant phase, which has lasted fifty-three years now, looks over at the front windows where Warren R. Kessler's Summer display is advancing upon Spring at a snail's pace. So Florene gets up stiffly and starts to box and shelve all the other black pumps that seem to be the losers of this here footwear free-for-all.

"Sweetie," says Beverly, "I could wear army boots to work, it wouldn't make one bit of difference. There's hardly anyone there. You've seen, our advertising barely fills a page now."

"Subscriptions?"

Beverly's rolled eyes and shooken head don't see much to that question. "Nobody wants a weekly newspaper."

"She won't go back to daily?"

"Honey, she had to cut her losses."

"What's she gonna do?"

"I don't think she's in any condition right now to give much thought to what she's gonna do."

"She still sleeping on their couch?"

"I doubt if she sleeps. Mr. H. is bad. He blames himself. He keeps saying it's all his fault. That Steve would never have been in that situation if it hadn't been for him."

"He was doing so well, up until." Florene drops sidesaddle upon the fitting stool to help Beverly back into her wedgies. "The day they came in together for new golf shoes, father-in-law and son-in-law, the one leading the other, was about the best thing I've ever seen, Bev."

And I think Florene's face suddenly turning emotional is about the hardest thing I've ever seen. She probly should have sprayed rain guard on Beverly's new shoes. It might be too late.

"Thirty minutes, tops," says Ray dabbing his eyes from the last flurry of yawns. "I did four chairs, two armoires and a coffee table."

"Couldn't you have taken something," says Milt, biting into his bear-claw like today for some reason Nickano decided to fry em in castor oil, "just this one time?"

"I don't wanna get hooked."

"You're weird, Goldie. Go to your room."

"Anyway, to get back to your original question," says Ray, very pale in his good black suit, "I think the family is the one that offers the reward. I don't think the sheriff can use taxpayer money for that."

"But twenty-five grand. That's small potatoes. Any leads in there, Bill?"

The spiffy and snazzy *Cottonwood Collaborator* is open on the table and Bill shakes his head. "Sheriff states that they've set up a toll free number for anyone that saw or knows anything concerning the incident or the description of the vehicle or identity of the driver. They know it was a large vehicle from the distance his body was thrown. But no skid marks, which indicates it did not slow down or attempt to avoid the victim." There's a light brown stain where Ray's unrested hand spilled coffee upon the small print that says "The *Cottonwood Collaborator* is a daily newspaper owned and operated by Beef Belt Consolidated News Corporation, a division of Euphemion Packing Company."

"But somebody had to have stopped and picked up his white cane. It was nowhere to be found."

"Why would anybody do that, Milt?" Milt gets that look a lot, with the comments he makes. It ain't just Ray. "That idea is sick, man. He didn't have the cane with him, maybe that's why he—"

"Well that makes even less sense," says Milt. "He always had the cane. Tap tap. Tap tap."

"I'm really not looking forward to this service," says Ray into his cold coffee cup.

"There's no burial, huh?" says Milt. "Just a service?"

Ray nods and Bill says it's like a memorial service with the family, and the three of them talk a little about what they probly did with the ashes and about Steve's folks and his son being here from Chicago and about Janet.

From the kitchen no whistling, humming, nor music whatsoever drifts abroad. Even the pots and pans is half-hearted in their pings and dings, with just a slow endless stirring in the background. Bill folds up the *Collaborator* and flings it into the corner of the booth where Kenny ain't sitting, or sneering, and where Kenny ain't sit or sneered for pert'ner going on ten months now.

Rookie sheriff's deputy Laertes Norris has stopped on the way to the church to scout around the taped-off area where one week ago he found his friend face-up on the gravel shoulder and can't recount too much about what happened after that cause he claims it's a blur and the few things that ain't blurred don't make no sense. He takes a slow walk down the unfinished roadside row of cottonwood seedlings that his friend had planted. He trails his hand lightly over each silver-green top. He looks over the planting tools, the bags of topsoil, the watering can and the unplanted seedlings in their plastic tubs. White chalk don't work on gravel so they used white spray paint instead and he tries not to look at that part of the scene.

And now as he rubs his jaw and appears to contemplate the riddles of life, Deputy Norris may also be mulling one of the pestering little riddles of this here dreadful death. But I can tell you: he ain't gonna find that white tapping cane.

See, I doubt very seriously that the law will ever catch up with the one who done this thing. That vehicle got clean away. Well, was it hit and run? Maybe it was, but then again: when you're driving a big rig semi tractor-trailer and you're turning sharp off East Highway 30 onto a side road southward bound, maybe you wouldn't even see a young feller crouched on the right shoulder feeling around with his hands for a spot to dig in. Maybe you wouldn't feel no impact. Maybe you drove on south none the wiser. But in one respect the reports is all wrong. There was other witnesses. A bunch in fact. The passengers: some of the passengers saw the whole thing. Sure, their eyes was big and froze with alarm and had nothing more than steel slats to see through, but they saw. And the final thing they saw was that white cane twirling through the air and landing smack on the roof of that there unheeding cattle truck.

Yet I don't guess none of them witnesses will give much testimony since they was enroute to a shiny new facility that promised to employ them on a short-term basis for nominal wages. And they was guaranteed by the management not to have to worry a bit about punching the clock on their way out.

I'll tell you someone else who needn't worry about punching that time clock. Or searching for convenient parking. Or paying his mortgage. That someone's new SUV has a reserved spot in the rear where the door says Euphemion Management Only and the sign above the SUV says Reserved for Kendall Smold, Chief of Sales. Who can smile any way he wants. Come and go as early or late as he wants, since sales has took off like a bunch of well-fed sandhill cranes. Not that you'd see any such noble wingspreads around here these days. There's dang few fish in this stretch of river since the gray foamy runoff begun in January.

Now, signwise, they've got a real classy one out front. Framed in actual cottonwood with a fine photo of Old Grateful and some nice words of tribute to her life and how she guided and inspired for pert'ner four hundred years. Euphemion themselves footed the bill for that beautiful sign. Not more than eighty, ninety feet from the exact spot where the old gal stood and reigned over this valley. The exact spot where now parades the marvel of modern advancement as animal after animal is hung by the hooves, whisked through a dizzy maze and before they know it they're a chewy succulent roast in clear plastic.

Don't think that one swanky sign is all the memory of Old Grateful that's left. For one thing, Keith come back from photography school in Kearney to do a study in black and white of O.G. and her shapely entourage. Before they was chainsawed. He give the photos to the high school to hang in their auditorium. And another set to the probation department, maybe in the hopes of being let off early. Most important of all he emailed a set to Tanya at the university as she sat the lone freshman in her Friday morning class, Demographic History of the Central Asian Steppe, since Tanya didn't have a lick of trouble testing out of all the interductory history classes.

The other thing is Professor Tinker made em cut a cross-section out of O.G.'s middle and Ray polished and varnished it to perfection one night and now it's on display at the County Historical Society. Along with the skeleton of a big wolf-like dog that was dug up when they was puttin in the drainage ducts by the river.

"We can put you in Room one ten," says Lyle to the nice folks who just come from the memorial service and don't especially feel like driving all the way back to Omaha tonight. "That's the last room I've got. In fact, that was his room when he first arrived in town." You know, come to think, it's always kinda cool in this motel lobby. Folks can't help but shiver. Even Lyle sometimes.

I'll tell ya, never has Lyle Griff looked so sad turning on his No Vacancy sign.

The wind she's a busy gal this evening, out and about and sweeping through alleys and parks. Whistling whenever she can. Something kinda dire: one of them Russian overtures, I think. She's a classy gal, you know, travels quite extensively. Unlike yours truly. Old stick in the—nevermind.

Swarms of new-flung cottonwood seeds is swirling downwind by the river. Sure, it ain't quite what it was, absent them half dozen regal beauties. But here west of town it's a mild intermittent flurry. The river's high and cold, given the season. The blankets is green. Treetops full and bright. Whenever the Wind comes they give her a standing ovation. But for that and the river's rush, it's as quiet as you'd want. Still, folks was here, not so very long ago. Five, maybe six, sets of muddy footprints is freshly huddled here upon the riverbank. One set of prints: a women's size 8B running shoe. Last year's model that Florene would recognize right off, and them's the ones that clumb down and back to the very water's edge. Leaving a trail of fine white ash in their wake.

Well, they drift and hover in curious flighty capers and by and by a gang of them cottony seedlets decide to light in some of these here mudprints. Tickles a bit when they stick. Not too very awful. Them seeds love ash, you know, that's nourishment to them.

Can't promise nothing. I'll do what I can.

Readers Guide

1. Who is the narrator of the two stories (the Native American story and the modern story)? What clues helped you figure out his identity?

2. Why do you think he was chosen to tell the stories?

3. Did you like the way the two stories were interwoven, so to speak? Why or why not?

4. How were the two stories connected historically, if at all? What ideas was the author trying to illustrate by such connections, if any?

5. Besides historical connections, did you see any parallels or contrasts between the Native American story and the modern day story? What social or political opinions do you think the author was attempting to express? How do you feel about these issues?

6. When Lark ran away from her village, was she acting selflessly, selfishly, or do you think it may have been a mixture of the two?

7. What were Steve's reasons for coming to Cottonwood? What do you think his initial impression of Janet was? And her initial impression of him?

8. What does Janet mean when she storms out of the Grouse Club, telling Steve he has his script all ready for the City Council meeting? Why does she react with anger? What deeper issues underlie all this anger?

9. Why did Tanya ask Keith to take a contest photo of the cottonwoods? What was her motive? Why didn't she take the photo herself?

10. Why did Steve try to cover up the attempted robbery and shooting outside the supermarket? Was the cover-up the only reason Janet was upset when she found out?

11. How do animals figure into the stories? Are they important?

12. Do you think there was any mutual attraction between Lark and Red Moon before circumstances literally threw them together at the climax on the scaffold? Do you think there is any chance they will ever be able to make a life together?

13. If there were a sequel to this book, how do you imagine the story would continue?

CPSIA information can be obtained
at www.ICGtesting.com
Printed in the USA
BVHW07s1803200618
519524BV00013BA/878/P